Come Home With Us

Come Home With Us

Rob Matthews

Seattle, WA

Fanny Press
PO Box 70515
Seattle, WA 98127

For more information go to: www.fannypress.com

Cover design by Sabrina Sun

Come Home With Us
Copyright © 2016 by Rob Matthews

ISBN: 978-1-60381-399-0 (Trade Paper)
ISBN: 978-1-60381-452-2 (eBook)

Printed in the United States of America

Chapter One

~

'ANYTHING?' SHE ASKED.
'Not yet,' I said, trying to keep the desperation out of my voice.

'Don't you want to be inside me?'

'More than anything.'

'Imagine how good it will feel.'

'Maybe I'm just too tired.'

'That's a shame. Because, Rob, I've been a bad girl.'

For the first time that evening, my cock twitched. 'What have you done?'

'I was at work when I got an email from Darrell. He said he needed to have an urgent meeting with me in the parking garage.'

'Strange place for a meeting.'

'He was waiting for me in his car. I got into the passenger seat. He didn't say anything. He just unzipped his pants. I started to say, "What if someone sees?" But when I saw his cock, that beautiful black cock, I couldn't resist. I just put my lips around it.'

'Is it bigger than mine?'

'You know it is, babe. It's three inches longer and *so* much thicker. I moved my mouth up and down on it. He was getting more and more turned on. But he wasn't as excited as I was. Then he made this noise and I knew what was going to happen next. He filled my mouth with his hot cum. It tasted so good. It was like honey. I sat up, shaking with lust for him. I said, "Now what are you going to do for me?" He just laughed and said, "Do I look like the kind of guy who eats pussy? Get back to work." I ran back upstairs and locked myself in the bathroom.'

I put her hand on my cock. She grinned when she felt how hard it was. 'Did you make yourself cum?' I asked her.

'Oh babe, I came so hard, I had to stop myself from screaming.'

I reached for the pack of condoms on the bedside table and put one on. 'What were you thinking about when you came?'

'I was imagining Darrell using that big hard cock to fuck me properly.'

I got on top of her. 'Has he ever fucked you?'

'No. I keep begging him to. But he's got a girlfriend and he wants to be faithful to her. He says cumming in my mouth isn't cheating.'

She reached down and fed my cock into her cunt.

'Why don't you think about him now?' I said.

'It's all I *can* think about.' As I started to move inside her, she closed her eyes and moaned, 'Oh, fuck me, Darrell.'

Hearing my wife say another man's name was too much for me. I tensed my muscles, trying to make it last a few seconds more. But I couldn't stop myself. She felt me cumming into the condom. She sighed quietly. I knew she was disappointed. But, fortunately for her, I *am* the kind of guy who eats pussy.

Tina had three lovers in those days. Darrell was her favorite. There was also Andrew, a shy twenty-one year old, who had been a virgin when he first arrived in her office. But as she often told me, 'He's definitely not a virgin now.' And there was Ginny from HR. At the office party one Christmas, Tina and Ginny had drunk too much champagne. Even though they were both married and had always considered themselves straight, they'd ended up experimenting in the stationery cupboard. They'd been experimenting together ever since.

Man or woman, black or white, Tina had wide-ranging tastes in sexual partners. But Darrell, Andrew, and Ginny all had one important thing in common: none of them existed outside our fantasies. Tina and I enjoyed fantasizing but we'd always promised to be completely faithful to each other.

Then, one Monday evening in January, everything changed.

'The program's starting!' shouted Tina from the den.

I was in the kitchen, straining spaghetti. 'I'll be there in a minute,' I shouted back. 'Which wine did you go with?'

'Cabernet Sauvignon, 2012.'

'That was a good year for the Cabernet.'

'Like you have any idea.'

I ran into the den with two steaming plates of pasta. 'Saucepan to plate in twelve point four seconds,' I said, proudly. 'A new record.'

'That deserves a kiss.' I sat down beside her on the couch.

'Absolutely.' She kissed me. 'And a glass of Cabernet.'

'Cheers,' I said, clinking my glass against hers.

'Cheers. Now watch the program.'

'What have I missed?'

'A man is walking through the woods late at night. Someone is watching him with night vision goggles. I do not ….'

I joined in. It was our catchphrase when watching crime dramas. 'I do not have high hopes for his future!'

When the program was over, Tina switched off the TV. We sat back on the couch with our glasses. 'How was work?' I asked her.

'David's been on my case all day. He wants me to work with this new guy in Spain. He says it will be good for me to get some international experience.'

'Do you think you'll have to go to Spain sometime?'

'It's possible.'

'Great. If you can take a few vacation days while you're there, I'll see if I can come over at the same time.'

She sighed. 'If I haven't quit by then. David wants me to carry on with all the U.S. stuff at the same time. It was constant today. Every time I gave him something on Spain, he said, "And what's happening with the guys in Chicago?" So I told him what was happening with the guys in Chicago and immediately, it was, "Here's another thing I need you to do for Spain". It's a good thing Steve was there. He's had his own problems with David, so we amused ourselves by plotting our revenge.'

'What did you come up with?'

'I wanted to go with the old sugar in the gas tank routine. But Steve read somewhere that that doesn't actually work. So I suggested putting a rattlesnake in David's bed. Then we decided no one deserves to share a bed with David, not even a rattlesnake.'

'I'm sure his wife loves sharing a bed with him.'

'Or maybe she just cuddles up with his bank statement. I met his wife at the company picnic. She's gorgeous. We can't understand how she ended up with David. I told Steve she should appear in a public service ad saying, "This is who I married – and that's why you shouldn't do drugs."'

'What did Steve say to that?'

'He said he'd run my daily reports, so I could concentrate on what David wanted.'

'Bless him.'

'I've told Steve he can never quit. I think I'd go crazy without him. How was your day?'

'I asked one of my students what "firework" meant. She said, "It is the fantastic work done by the brave men and women of our fire service. Knowing they are out there, I sleep well in my bed." She was so passionate about it, I didn't have the heart to tell her she was wrong.'

Tina laughed. 'Have you got to work this evening?'

'I've got a few assignments I should mark. Nothing that can't wait, though. What about you?'

'I need your help with something, if that's okay. I was feeling a bit down after work so I went to Victoria's Secret and bought a whole lot of different bras and panties. I don't know what looks best on me. I'll have to try all of them on and you can help me decide.'

'It's a dirty job.'

'I'm hoping it's going to be very dirty,' she said, with one of her wicked grins. 'But before we do that, can I ask you something? You know when we're in bed, we like to talk .... We love sharing fantasies about me with other people.'

I liked the way the conversation was going. I hoped she had a new fantasy she wanted to share. 'Oh yes!'

'I was wondering if that's all they are – just fantasies.'

'I always assumed so.'

'And do you think it's best to keep it that way?'

'Well ... I ... I don't know.' My heart was suddenly beating very fast. 'Why? Have you ... done something?'

'No. Well, not really. I would never do anything like that without talking to you first.' She paused and took a big gulp of wine. 'And that's why I'm talking to you now.'

I realized I was shaking. 'What do you mean?'

'First, let me say that I am totally in love with you, Rob. When I was young, I always said I'd never get married. I couldn't face being tied to the same person for the rest of my life. Then I met you and all that changed. When we got married, I was sure I'd never have sex with another man again. And I've been perfectly happy about that for the last fifteen years ....'

'Is the next word going to be "but"?'

She nodded. 'But a couple of days ago something happened.'

'What?'

'Someone at work did something – something that might be called flirting or might be called something else. At first, I figured it was nothing and I didn't think much about it. But the mind does funny things when you get bored at work. I started wondering what it would be like to kiss him and touch him and ….' She stopped and looked at me. 'Are you okay?'

'Yes,' I said.

'Do you want me to stop talking about this?'

'No, I'm fine.'

'To start with, it was just a daydream, like wondering what it would be like to walk on the moon. Nice to think about, but you know it's never going to happen. But there is a spark between him and me. I haven't felt that sort of electricity since … well, since I met you. Like I say, I'm totally in love with you. Nothing's going to change that. But it was kind of nice to have those feelings again. It was exciting. And that's when I thought I'd better talk to you.'

'We are talking about Steve, aren't we?'

'That obvious?'

' "Steve was great today!" and "I couldn't have made it through the week without Steve!" '

'That could just mean I admire his professionalism in the office.'

'Yeah, right.'

'If you think it's better that we keep this as a fantasy, just say so. Steve can join Darrell, Andrew, and Ginny in the imaginary lovers' club. But,' she looked at me steadily, 'if we ever want to do this in real life, this might be our chance.'

'You think he's attracted to you?'

'I could be misreading the signs, but I'm pretty sure he is.'

'He flirts with you?'

'Yes.'

'And you flirt back?'

'Yes.'

She put her hand on mine and squeezed it. I looked up at the picture on the wall. It was of Tina and me on our honeymoon in Rome. A street photographer had said we were the most perfect couple he'd ever seen. He just had to capture us. We were holding hands with the Colosseum in the background.

Tina followed my gaze and guessed my thoughts. 'I know there's a big difference between fantasy and reality,' she said.

'Just the thought of you flirting with another guy in the office is exciting. I want to hear a lot more about that later. But right now, I'm trying to think with my head – the one on my shoulders.'

'Don't worry. Whatever we decide to do, I will talk about Steve when we're in bed tonight. I promise to make you jealous as hell.'

'I guess I'm pretending to be him tonight.'

She gave me another of her wicked grins. 'I've been pretending you were him for some time now, babe!'

'If we do this,' I said with a tentative smile, 'it'll be a huge turn-on. But then it's still going to be in our lives when we're not turned on anymore. When we wake up on Monday morning and have to drive to work in the rain, you'll still have had sex with another man.'

She shrugged. 'Why should that be a problem? I mean, how many men did I have before I met you?'

'Eight.'

'And how many women did you have before you met me?'

'Just one.'

'And has that ever caused a problem between us?'

'We've talked about it often enough.'

'Only in bed. Never when we're having a fight.'

'But this is a bit different. Remember that day when you wore the pretty dress and all our family and friends were there? What did the minister say? "What God has joined, men must not divide." '

'No man's going to divide us, Rob.'

'We made a commitment when we got married.'

'And we're still going to be totally committed to each other.'

'Then there's the other issue,' I said with a frown. 'You don't dip your pen in the company inkwell.'

'It would be more like dipping the company pen in my inkwell. But I know what you mean. It's just that we've always fantasized about me seducing guys at work. It seemed the natural place to look.'

'You're not his boss, are you?'

'No. Carol's his boss. He works *with* me every day, but he doesn't work *for* me. And we'll make it clear to him that it's a casual thing. Just a bit of fun.'

I wasn't sure that my wife having sex with another man would ever be a casual bit of fun. 'So how do you see this happening?' I asked.

'We need to talk about that. I was thinking Steve and I could go off somewhere. I like the idea of going somewhere cheap – even a bit sleazy. Maybe a motel out of town. And then I'd come back home to you. My hair would be all messed up and my lipstick would be smeared. We'd get into bed and I'd tell you the whole story. Just imagine how much more exciting it would be, knowing that this adventure really happened and every word was true. You'd have the best cum of your life.'

'Yes, I would. But that's not what I want.'

'What do you want, babe?'

'I want to be there.'

'You want to be in the motel room with us? You want to watch me getting fucked?'

'Yes. But won't the desk clerk wonder what we're doing – three of us checking in to one room?'

'Rob, I love you, but you're the worst over-thinker I've ever met. The desk clerk won't give a damn what we're doing. He'll hand over the key and go back to watching the game. If he thinks about us at all, he'll just think I'm a complete slut.' She grinned. 'And I know you like me to be a bit slutty.'

'What will you be wearing?'

'How about my denim skirt with the brown leather boots and the matching brown tank top? You once said I could seduce anyone in that outfit.'

'What would you wear under it?'

'Why would I wear anything under it? But we're losing focus, babe. Come on.'

'Sorry. We'd have to go to a place where nobody knows us.'

'Yes. We'd have to drive a long way. But I like that idea. Imagine driving along, knowing what we're going to do when we arrive – the delicious anticipation. And then, afterwards, we wouldn't let ourselves talk about it on the way home. We'd make ourselves wait – the even more delicious frustration. And when we got home, you'd have to fuck me. You'd have to claim me back and prove you're as good as him.'

'Let's do it,' I said.

'You mean that?'

'Yes.'

'We're really going to do this?' She put her arms around my neck and kissed me. 'You're a wonderful husband, Rob. Do you want to go to bed now?'

'Like you wouldn't believe!'

We ran upstairs, tore off our clothes and got into bed. But she knew I didn't want to touch her yet. She lay beside me and asked, 'Now, what do you want to know about this new man in our life?'

'You said he did something that could be called flirting. What did he do?'

'Well, he's been complimenting me ever since he arrived. He's always saying I'm the prettiest girl in the office.'

'I can't argue with him there.'

Tina is very pretty and sexy. She has shoulder-length brown hair she ties into a respectable looking knot for work, but when she's going out, she wears it spiked up like a porcupine's quills. Her dark eyes sparkle with intelligence and humor. She has a strong, prominent nose and a smile that can be warm, playful, or wicked. She still has a great body at thirty-six—natural 34C breasts and a taut stomach. The hours on the stepper at the gym have given her well-toned thighs and calves. She sometimes complains that her ass is too big, but to me, those beautifully rounded cheeks are perfect.

'What really got me thinking was something he did a couple of days ago,' she said. 'I was sitting at my desk, showing him some figures on my computer, so he was standing very close to my chair. I glanced up and saw that he wasn't looking at the screen. He was looking down my blouse.'

'Which blouse were you wearing?'

'The red one.'

'That's quite low cut.'

'I acted like I hadn't noticed. But I kept pointing at the screen to make my blouse open up a bit more.'

'What did he see?'

'He got a perfect view of my cleavage and most of my right boob – inside my bra, of course. But I was wearing one of my white lace bras. They don't leave much to the imagination. He could pick my right nipple out of a line-up.'

I was breathing heavily. My heart was pounding. I'd heard Tina talk about her wild times with Darrell, Andrew, and Ginny. And I'd always loved her stories. But I'd always known they were just fantasies. Her talk about Steve glimpsing her boobs was tame by comparison. But it was so much more erotic because it was true.

'Does he know you're married?'

'Of course. I've told him all about you.'

'And he still looked?'

'Yes.'

'And you let him look?'

'I enjoyed him looking. I wanted to show him more. But there are some things you can't do in the office.'

'What is it about him that you like so much?'

'Well, he's very good looking. Short dark hair, deep brown eyes. He's one of those guys who always has the beginning of a beard no matter how often he shaves. That gives him a bit of a bad boy look. I love that.'

'But I don't look like that.'

'I know, babe. Why do you think I'm looking elsewhere? He's twenty-seven. So he's ten years younger than you. That helps. And he spends a lot of time in the gym. That helps too.' She paused and smiled. 'That helps a lot.'

'Has he got a better body than me?'

'Let's see.' She squeezed my bicep. 'His arms are a lot bigger and stronger than yours. He's got beautiful muscular shoulders that show through his shirt. You couldn't stop him fucking me even if you wanted to. But the best thing about him is his six pack.'

'You've seen it?'

'Oh yes. We were all at lunch one day. The guys were talking about whether you need to do crunches to get a decent six pack. Steve just lifted up his shirt and said, "I've never done a crunch in my life – this is all from cardio." '

'What did you see?'

'The best abs, ever. I wanted to kiss every part of his six pack. But I couldn't. So I went into the bathroom and … thought about him.'

'You mean you got yourself off?'

'What do you think?'

'Were you very wet?'

'My pussy was liquid.'

I put my hand between her legs. 'Just like it is now.'

'You know what to do, then.'

I got out of bed and switched off the light. When I got back in, I didn't say anything. I knew she wanted me to pretend to be Steve, but I had no idea how he spoke or what sort of things he would say, and I didn't want to spoil the fantasy. I thought that if he'd been attracted to Tina for some time, he'd be desperate to get inside her. He wouldn't spend too much time on foreplay. I ran my hands over her body. When my fingers stroked her nipples, I could almost believe I was Steve touching them for the first time. She sighed contentedly as I traced a line down her body and found her clit. I decided he wouldn't wait any longer. Rolling a condom onto my cock, I got on top of her and fucked her with the urgent thrusts of a man who had finally gotten what he wanted. I guessed that, in her dreams, Steve fucked her long and hard. I wanted to make that come true for her now. But I was too turned on. It took me less than a minute to cum. I went down and started licking her. I still imagined I was Steve, finally licking the cunt of the sexiest girl in the office. My tongue was as urgent as my cock had been. I flicked the tip of my tongue from side to side over her clit. As she came, she moaned, 'Oh Steve, you're so much better than my husband.'

Afterwards, she lay in my arms, the way she always did. 'Are you okay?' she asked.

'I'm fine,' I said. I was back to being me. Steve had vanished as soon as we'd both cum.

'You still want to go ahead?'

'Yes.'

'Are you sure?'

'Yes.'

'I'll talk to him tomorrow.' She turned over and went to sleep. I didn't get to see what she'd bought at Victoria's Secret.

I lay awake for a long time. When Tina had asked, 'Are you sure?' I'd said yes. But the truth is I wasn't sure anymore. My hormones had ebbed away as soon as I'd cum. As I lay there with my wife in my arms, I wanted to keep her all to myself. Sharing her was definitely something to be kept as a fantasy. Was I being selfish? I knew she loved me, but I also knew I didn't satisfy her. Tina was a passionate woman. She needed to be fucked properly. And I just couldn't do that for her.

No one would guess that from looking at me. I don't look like a natural born cuckold. I'm six foot two with light brown hair and hazel eyes. I don't have modeling agencies fighting over me, but I'm not bad-looking. I play tennis at least once a week so I'm in pretty good shape for someone my age. My cock is a respectable seven inches when fully erect. I may not be cut out for a career as a porn star, but I've got no complaints about its size. The first time Tina saw my cock, she gave it a squeeze and told it, 'You and I are going to have a lot of fun together.' She was disappointed when our first time lasted twelve seconds, but she was understanding. She even said with some pride that guys often had trouble controlling themselves on their first time with her. She said the next time would be better. But it wasn't. It never got much better.

Even so, we were married just over a year after we got together. Some people said we were rushing it. But it was the right thing to do. We loved each other's company. We enjoyed doing the same things. We could talk for hours about serious things or stupid things. It seemed obvious that we were meant to be together. She was still worried about our sex life but she said it would improve after we got married. Once I had the reassurance of knowing she was committed to me for life, I'd be more relaxed. But nothing changed. She had her fair share of orgasms, but I always needed to use my tongue, my fingers or a toy. She never got a hard cock that kept on fucking her until she was completely satisfied. I knew that was what she craved.

Could I deny her the chance of getting what she really wanted? Could I show her how much I loved her by standing aside and letting another man have sex with her? At two o'clock in the morning, the idea wasn't very appealing.

Chapter Two

~

Tꜱᴇ ɪᴅᴇᴀ ᴏꜰ ᴡᴀᴛᴄʜɪɴɢ my wife have sex with another man was even less appealing when I woke up. It was a freezing Tuesday morning in January. Every cell in my body was telling me to stay in bed. But we had to get up and go to work. I made coffee and toast while Tina was in the shower.

We sat on the couch and ate breakfast. I was tired and had a bit of a headache from the wine. A couple of years ago, I could have sat up drinking until three in the morning and still gotten up for work all bushy-tailed. Those days were definitely gone. Tina, on the other hand, was just as enthusiastic as she'd been the night before.

'What do you think I should say to Steve?'

I shrugged. 'You know him.'

'It's quite a difficult thing to work into conversation in the office. "Do you have last month's figures and do you want to screw me while my husband watches?" '

'Don't talk to him in the office, then. Ask him if he wants to go for a drink after work.'

'That's a good idea. Neutral ground.'

'Start by talking about the time he looked down your blouse.

He might be a bit embarrassed, but you can say you didn't mind him looking. Ask him if he'd like to see a bit more. Keep it light and breezy. Be ready to turn it into a joke if he's not interested.'

'Do you think he will be interested?'

'I've never met the guy. But there's a big difference between having a quick look down someone's blouse and—'

'We'll see what he says.'

We went to work. Since I arrived at the language school with half an hour to spare before my first lesson, I went to the teachers' lounge for a cup of coffee.

Danielle, the French teacher, was sitting by the window, marking assignments. 'Hey, Rob, how you doing?' she said. She prides herself on her idiomatic English.

'Pretty good. You?'

'I have cold.'

'Do you mean you *are* cold? Or do you mean have *a* cold?' She'd made me promise to correct her mistakes.

'I *am* cold. It is never like this at the south of France.'

'*In* the south of France.'

She clicked her tongue, annoyed with herself. 'What did you do last evening?'

Oh, nothing much. We talked over the idea of my wife having sex with one of her colleagues, but apart from that, it was fairly average. What I really said was, 'We just had a bite to eat and then went to bed. What about you?'

'I was so cold, I went to bed first then had a bite to eat after. I like breakfast in bed. I do not like supper in bed.'

'It's not so bad if you've got a TV in your bedroom.'

'I have a TV in front of my bed. It's strange. In France, we never have a TV in the bedroom. We are too busy with other things.'

I sometimes wondered if Danielle was flirting with me. But I thought it more likely she was just being French. My first lesson was teaching professional English to a group of Japanese businessmen. When I was actually teaching, I was focused on the job. But when the students were doing exercises, my mind wandered.

My internal dialogue went like this:

'I should call Tina now and tell her not to talk to Steve. No good can come of this.'

'But Tina's very keen. She obviously likes this Steve guy. Wouldn't you rather she was honest with you and made you a part of it instead of having an affair behind your back?'

'Why would she have an affair? She loves me.'

'Yes, she does. But let's face it, you're not giving her what she needs. You're lucky if you can last two minutes most nights.'

'Well, maybe if we didn't spend all our time talking about her screwing around, I wouldn't be so turned on and I'd last a bit longer.'

'But that turns her on as well. Imagine how much more excited she'll be if it's actually happening.'

'And it'll be such a turn-on for me too.'

'But what about afterwards? Why would she come back to you after that? Do you think she'll be happy with you when she's had something so much better?'

'Yes, you're right. I should call Tina now and tell her—'

'Are you going to evaluate our working, professor?' asked an insurance broker from Kyoto.

'Yes, sorry,' I said and got my mind back on the job.

At eleven o'clock, I gave the students fifteen minutes to get coffee and checked my phone. There was a message from Tina, *Steve ok 4 drink 2nite. Wish me luck.*

Part of me still wanted to text her back saying, *Don't do it! Just come home!* Instead, I wrote, *Hope everything goes well.*

A second later, my phone beeped again. *Get wine a chillin!*

WHEN I GOT HOME that evening, I put a bottle into the fridge. And then I waited. I had no idea how long Tina's talk with Steve would take. Was she going to spend a long time building up to it? Or would she just come right out and ask him? I tried to read a book but couldn't keep my eyes on the page. I washed the dishes from breakfast. That took five minutes. Then I waited a bit longer. Something told me I'd better get used to this. Cuckolds probably spent a lot of time sitting home alone. A thought crept into my mind. Maybe they'd decided to go ahead without me. They could have just gone back to his place. Maybe she'd come home at midnight, smelling of his cologne. My cock stirred at the thought. What stories would she have to tell me when she got home? But then my cock shriveled at the next thought. Maybe she wouldn't come home at all.

It was a relief when I heard her key in the door. I went out to the hall, trying to look relaxed. I didn't want her to know I'd been worrying.

'Hey, babe,' she said. Her lipstick wasn't smeared. Her hair wasn't messed up.

'How are you?'

'It's been an interesting evening. How about that drink?'

I got the bottle out of the fridge and took two glasses from the cupboard. When I came back into the hall, she'd taken off her coat. She was wearing a white blouse with a neckline that plunged down to show two inches of cleavage. 'Nice top,' I said. 'I've never seen that one before.'

'I had to buy it at lunchtime. I sent Steve an email this morning, asking him if he wanted to come for a drink. He wrote back immediately saying yes. Then I realized I wasn't exactly dressed for seduction. It was so cold this morning, I went out wearing my big thick sweater. So I had to run out and buy this.'

'And ... err ... did it work?' I asked tentatively.

'Pour me a glass and I'll tell you all about it.' We went into the den and sat down on the couch. 'I didn't want to go to the bar near the office. Everyone from work goes there. The last thing I wanted was David listening in. So I suggested going to a place a few blocks away. Steve bought the drinks. We sat and talked about work. He wanted to let off steam. He said that David hadn't given him a straight answer all day. Every time he asked a question, David just said, "What do you think?" or "Based on your experience, what would you do?" When you consider how much David gets paid, you'd think—'

'What did you talk about besides David?'

'Yes, sorry. I did what you suggested. I talked about that time he looked down my blouse. He went a bit red, but he knew he wasn't in trouble. If I'd wanted to tell him off, I'd have done it in the office. I was trying to be breezy like you said so I just asked, "See anything you like?" He smiled and said, "A couple of things caught my eye." So I asked him if he'd like to see a bit more some time. I said it with a big grin so I could turn it into a joke if I had to. He was grinning too, but it was a nervous grin. The poor guy really wasn't sure what was happening. He said, "Obviously I'd love to but …" and he pointed at my wedding ring. Then it was really make or break time. I said, "Yes, I am married. But my husband and I have always fantasized about him watching me with another guy." Then I asked him straight out if he would consider being that other guy.'

'What did he say to that?'

'He took a very big gulp of his drink and said, "Wow." He didn't say anything else for a while and I sat there, holding my breath. Did he mean, "Wow, that sounds great"? Or did he mean, "Wow, I can't believe you asked me something like that; wait till David hears about this"? Then he asked me how it would work. I said it would just be a casual thing. I told him I love you very much and would never do anything to harm our relationship. He said he was fine with that. He broke up with his last girlfriend a couple of months ago and he's not looking to get into anything serious. I talked about our plan for going to a motel. But he didn't like that idea. He spent too much time in motels when he was a kid on family holidays. To him, a motel room means six people fighting to get into the bathroom and his brother snoring in the bed next to him. That doesn't exactly turn him on. So he suggested coming here.'

'Here?'

'What's wrong with that?'

'In our home?'

Tina gave me a look. 'You don't want him entering your house but you're fine with him entering your wife?'

'I suppose it could be here. It's just that, in our fantasies, it's always been at work or in a hotel room or on a beach.'

'This isn't a fantasy anymore.'

'So what did you say?'

'I said I didn't think that would be a problem. And then he said he's free on Friday.'

'This Friday?'

'Yes.'

'And what did you say?'

'I said I thought we were free as well. We are, aren't we?'

I felt my stomach drop. It reminded me of the time I went skydiving. I'd always said I wanted to try it some time. So, for my thirtieth birthday, my parents bought me a skydiving experience. As I stood at the open hatchway of the plane, I realized this was no longer something that was going to happen sometime. It was going to happen now. I looked down and saw the ground a very long way below me. Skydiving suddenly seemed like a really stupid thing to do. And now I felt like I was standing at another open hatchway. My wife wouldn't be having sex with another man at some vague point in the future. She'd be doing it in three days' time. I was about to jump into the world of cuckoldry. And just then, it also seemed like a really stupid thing to do. But I didn't want to wimp out of the skydive. So I jumped. I didn't want to wimp out of this, either. So I said, 'Yes, we're free on Friday.'

Chapter Three

~

I GOT HOME AT six on Friday evening. The den was a mess. The dirty plates from last night's dinner were still on the floor. I took them into the kitchen and washed them. I was just straightening up the pile of magazines on Tina's side of the couch when my phone beeped. It was a text from Tina, *Problem at work. Home asap but no idea when.*

I needed to keep busy to stop myself from thinking too much. So I cleaned. I ran the vacuum over the den carpet. I swept the kitchen floor, dusted the bookshelves and polished the bathroom mirror. The whole house was looking good by the time I heard Tina's key in the door. I looked at my watch. It was just coming up to nine o'clock. I took a deep breath and went out to the hall. Tina was taking off her coat. She was alone.

'Where is he?' I asked.

'And hello to you,' she replied.

'Sorry. Hello.'

'He had a couple of things he needed to finish up.'

'So he's not coming?'

'He said he'd be right behind me.' We went into the den. 'Have you been cleaning?'

'Just a bit.'

'I don't think he's going to be worried about the state of our house. In fact, I'll be quite upset if that's what he focuses on.'

'He's still a guest.'

'Oh well, it looks better than it has in months. Do you want a drink?'

'I'm okay for the moment.'

'I think I'd better have one.'

'Tina, if you don't want to do this, we can still call it off.'

'No, I'm fine. I just want to relax a bit. It's been a hellish day at work. We had these figures that absolutely had to be sent to the client tonight. I thought surely they could wait until Monday. But David said the client *might* want to look at them over the weekend. So we worked half the night on the off chance that—'

'I was just wondering if there might be a better time to do this.'

'What, when Venus is in the cusp of Aquarius? Or when thirteen white doves fly past in the shape of a cross? Rob, either we're going to do this or we're not.'

'I know. It's just—'

The doorbell rang.

'Well, it's too late to worry about it now,' she said. 'Are you ready?'

'I don't know.'

She went to open the door. I had no idea how Steve and I were going to talk to each other. What do you say to the man who's come over to fuck your wife? Maybe he despised me. Maybe he was going to stride in, sneering, 'You pathetic loser, I'm here to satisfy Tina because you can't. Kiss my boots and beg me to fuck her.' While this was going through my head, I tried to find a nonchalant way of standing. I couldn't find one, so I tried a nonchalant way of sitting. I was failing at that too when they came in. 'Steve, this is my husband, Rob.'

He stepped forward and shook my hand. 'Good to meet you.'

'You too, Steve. I've heard a lot about you.'

'Nice house.'

'Thank you. Any trouble finding it?'

'No. Tina drew me a map. It was very clear.'

'I hear you had some trouble at work this evening.'

'That's right,' he said. 'We had to get something to a client tonight. So, of course, the email system went down.'

'What system do you use?'

'Outlook.'

'That's what we use at the language school.'

'Really? Tina didn't mention it.'

'I don't think I ever told Tina.' I turned to her. 'Did I ever tell you that we use Outlook?'

'No, babe, you didn't. And we always said there'd be no secrets between us.'

'We've been using it for some time,' I continued. 'And we've always found it very reliable.'

'Generally, it's reliable for us too,' said Steve. 'Just today—'

'Why don't we …?' began Tina.

'So, any plans for the weekend?' I asked Steve.

'Not much. Up early to play tennis tomorrow.'

'Oh, I play tennis too.'

'Really? We must have a game some time.'

'That would be great.'

Tina tried again. 'Steve, why don't you—?'

'Could I use your bathroom?' he asked.

'Sure,' I said. 'Up the stairs. First on the left.'

He went upstairs. Tina gave me a look. 'What are you doing, Rob?' she asked in a low voice.

'What do you mean?'

'All that crap about emails and tennis?'

'Well, that's one of the differences between fantasy and reality. Fantasies start at the good bit. In reality, you've got to build up to it.'

'You've built up enough now.'

'I suppose so.'

I must have sounded nervous because Tina asked, 'Are you okay?'

'I'm fine.'

She kissed me and whispered in my ear, 'There's a man right here in our house. He's not here to talk. He's here to fuck me. And you're going to watch him do it. Isn't that what you want? Because it's definitely what I want. I've been dreaming about it all day.' She sat down on the couch and undid the top two buttons of her blouse. Steve came downstairs. 'Steve,' said Tina, 'why don't you come and sit next to me? Rob, maybe you could get us some drinks.'

I went into the kitchen and got a bottle of white wine out of the fridge. It felt strange, reaching into the cupboard for three glasses rather than two. I went back into the den, where Tina and Steve were sitting on the couch. They weren't doing or saying anything. He looked uncomfortable. I remembered all the fantasies where Tina had started with, 'I was in bed with this hot guy.' We had never thought to ask, 'How did you break the ice when he first arrived?' I poured us all some wine. We clinked our glasses together.

'I'm not sure what the rules are,' said Steve.

'I guess we make our own rules,' said Tina.

'Can I kiss you?'

'Maybe better not,' I said.

'Of course you can kiss me. I'm not a prostitute.' She gave him one of her wicked grins. 'But I am a bit of a whore.'

He put his hand behind her head and pulled her gently towards him. He kissed her on the lips. Her eyes closed. She put her arm around him. She ran her hand over the muscles in his shoulders. He moved his head away from hers. She opened her eyes and smiled. She leaned forward to show a little more cleavage. 'You recognize these?' she asked. He nodded. 'If you'd like to see some more, maybe we should take this upstairs.'

She stood up and started up the stairs. Steve followed, and I went up behind them, still holding my glass of wine. Tina has a way of wiggling her ass as she's going upstairs. She knows how much I love it. Only this time, she wasn't doing it for me.

She went into the bedroom and switched on the light. Standing by the bed, she started to unbutton her blouse. She did it slowly, lingering over each button. She enjoyed teasing him. Her blouse opened to reveal a simple white bra. She stopped for a moment to let him enjoy the anticipation. I held my breath. I'd seen Tina's breasts hundreds of times. But now I was about to see them through another man's eyes. She reached behind her back, unhooked the clasp of her bra, and let the garment fall away. And there they were. They were so beautiful – naturally round and firm with just a subtle darkening of shade at the nipple. I felt a mixture of emotions. I was proud that my wife was so beautiful and sexy. I was turned on by the sight of her taking off her clothes for another man. I was also jealous of him. A part of me wished he would go away and leave me alone with her. Tina let him look for a moment. 'Everything you expected?' she asked.

'All the times I've watched you in the office,' he said, 'I never imagined you had anything like that under your clothes.' He raised his hands towards her tits, but she pushed them away with a teasing smile.

'Your turn,' she said.

He didn't tease her. He unbuttoned his shirt quickly and threw it on the floor. I had to admit he was in good shape. He had a broad chest – tanned skin stretched across well-defined pecs. His shoulder muscles bulged up on either side of his neck. His arms were thick and strong. She ran her hands all over his chest and shoulders. She squeezed his arms and traced her fingers along the veins of his biceps. 'You've got the body I've always dreamed of,' she said. I wondered if she was saying this to make me jealous. I wanted her to look at me and give me one of her grins. But she didn't. I had to face the fact that she wasn't thinking about me at all just then.

'You like?' he asked.

She wasn't teasing anymore. She took off her trousers and panties. She stood in front of him, naked, with her legs slightly apart. She took his hand and put it between her legs. He smiled as he slid a finger into her cunt and felt just how wet she was for him. 'That's how much I like,' she said.

She got onto the bed. He gently positioned her on all fours, facing away from him. I saw something glint on her hand. The only thing she was wearing was her wedding ring. The symbol of her commitment to me was still on her finger as she parted her legs and waited for another man's cock. He took off his trousers and shorts. Tina was looking over her shoulder, trying to see his cock. I could see it better than she could. It wasn't the ten-incher of our fantasies. But it was long and thick. I guessed it was about eight and a half inches. It was definitely bigger than mine. He knelt up on the bed behind her and put his hands on her hips. Then he stopped and looked at me. For a second, I thought he was checking that I was still happy with the situation. Maybe he was even asking my permission. But he just said, 'Have you got any condoms?' I went round to my side of the bed and handed him one. I had a good view from the side of the bed, so I stayed there. I sat down with my back against the wall. I took a gulp of wine. There was no turning back now. Steve put on the condom. With the middle finger of his right hand, he found the entrance to her cunt. He used his finger to guide his cock into her. She gasped at the feel of him inside her. He was finding places I had never reached – places that hadn't been touched in years.

When he was all the way in, he stopped for a moment to enjoy the feel of my wife's hot, wet cunt around his cock. Then he pulled out until only the tip was inside her. The condom-covered shaft was glistening with her juices. He paused for a second, then he put his hands on her hips and thrust himself back into her as hard as he could. She screamed with both pleasure and surprise. He thrust into her again before she could catch her breath. Then he settled into a comfortable rhythm.

He was still fucking her hard but he concentrated on keeping up a steady pace, rather than making her scream with every thrust. Her head was on the pillow, her eyes closed. Her mouth was open and her forehead was shiny with sweat. She was lost in the moment, giving herself over to the sensations coursing through her body. She'd never looked like that with me. Her moans were getting louder and closer together. I could tell she was close to cumming.

He started to thrust more quickly. She was going to climax any second. Then he stopped. With just the tip of his cock still inside her, he waited. He didn't move at all.

'What's wrong?' asked Tina, breathlessly.

'Nothing,' he replied, calmly.

'Why have you stopped? I was almost there.'

'I know. I'm making you wait for it.'

'I need you to make me cum, you bastard!' she shouted. Her voice was hoarse with desire.

He started moving inside her again. She was still very close to cumming. Her gasps were building towards an orgasmic scream. I was sure that one more thrust would push her over the edge. But again he stopped and let the feeling subside. I watched him with a mixture of jealousy and awe. I have never made Tina cum using just my cock. If I thought there was any chance of bringing her to orgasm this way, I would take it immediately. But here he was, playing with her, teasing her. He was in charge. He knew he could make her cum whenever he chose.

'Please, Steve, please!' she cried out.

He started fucking her again. This time, he didn't stop or slow down as she got close to orgasm. Instead, he increased the speed of his thrusts. Tina took a deep breath. All her muscles tensed. Then she screamed. Her whole body shuddered as an orgasm ripped through her. Steve let out a triumphant 'Yeah!' With his cock still inside her, he waited for her breathing to become more regular. Then he started fucking her again. Now that she had cum, he could fuck her selfishly. He was focusing on his own pleasure.

I couldn't believe how much control he had. It was his first time with her. He'd been watching her in the office, feeling his desire for her build. He must have been fantasizing about her for weeks. And he was acting like he could cum any time he wanted. He thrust three more times. Then, with a low grunt of satisfaction, he came inside her.

He pulled out. She collapsed onto the bed. Her hair was plastered down with sweat, and she was panting. Steve sat down on the bed. She reached for his hand and squeezed it. 'Thank you,' she said.

It's what every man wants to hear – his wife thanking another man for fucking her.

Steve pulled off the condom. 'Have you got a tissue?' he asked me. I handed him the box.

Tina raised her head. 'Let me see.' He held up the condom. It was a quarter full. 'I could feel it pumping into the condom,' she said. 'I wish I could feel it pumping into me.' Steve wrapped the condom in a tissue and threw it into the wastepaper basket. 'Come here,' said Tina. He lay down next to her. She rested her head on his chest, and he put his arms around her. She was still breathing heavily. Gradually her breathing became more regular. Steve's breathing began to synchronize with hers. They closed their eyes. Soon they were both asleep.

This was not what I wanted at all. I wanted Steve to make his excuses and leave so I could be alone with Tina. I wanted to talk to her. I wanted her to pay attention to me again. But there was no sign of that happening. I was discovering another way in which fantasy and reality are different. Fantasies disappear when you've finished with them. They don't hang around and fall asleep in your bed.

I went downstairs. If I thought I was restless when I was waiting for Tina to come home, it was nothing to how I felt now. I looked at my watch. It was ten o'clock. I prowled from room to room. I couldn't sit down, and there was nothing left to clean. After ten minutes, I heard a creak from the bedroom.

Tina came softly down the stairs, wearing just her bathrobe. 'How are you doing, babe?' she whispered.

I didn't see any need to whisper. 'I'm fine, but—'

'Sh. Steve's asleep.'

'I know. In our bed. Does he think he's staying the night?'

She shrugged. 'It looks like it.'

'Didn't you tell him he's supposed to leave afterwards?'

'To be honest, I didn't really think about what was going to happen afterwards.'

'He's got to get up early tomorrow to play tennis. Has he even thought about that?'

'It's probably not the main thing on his mind right now.'

'And we haven't eaten.'

'You get something if you want. I'm not hungry.'

'Can't you just tell him to go?'

'That would be rude.'

'Rude?'

'Like you said, he's still a guest.'

'There isn't room for him to stay here.'

'He looks quite comfortable where he is.'

'So where are you going to sleep?'

For the first time that evening, she gave me one of her wicked grins. 'I'm going to sleep naked in my lover's arms.'

'And where am I going to sleep?'

'On the couch.'

'On the couch?'

'I think that's quite a turn-on. You're going to be down here on the couch. I'm going to be very comfortable in our bed, with Steve's big strong arms around me.'

'It's not much of a turn-on for me.'

She put her hand on my crotch. 'So why is your cock hard?' She kissed me. 'I love you. You do know that, don't you?'

'I love you too.'

'You have a good night, babe. I'll see you in the morning.' I watched her go upstairs, head into the bedroom, and close the door. I was more turned on than I'd ever been in my life. I didn't know what to do. I thought about jerking off. A feather landing on my cock would have made me cum at that moment. But I didn't touch it. I knew that, if I came, I wouldn't be turned on anymore. But the situation wouldn't have changed. I'd still be sleeping alone on the couch and Tina would still be upstairs in Steve's arms.

I took the spare blanket out of the airing cupboard. My pajamas were in the bedroom so I stripped down to my shorts and t-shirt and lay on the couch. It was great to sit on but I couldn't find a comfortable way of lying on it. Why had we turned this into reality? If we'd kept it as a fantasy, I'd be the one lying with Tina in my arms. But then I remembered watching her undressing for Steve. I remembered him gazing at my wife's tits. I thought about the way she looked at him, completely caught up in the moment. I remembered the way she screamed as he pushed his cock into her cunt. And I was so glad we'd turned it into reality.

I woke up when I felt Tina's hand on my shoulder. She was standing in front of the couch in her bathrobe. 'Morning, babe,' she said. I sat up so she could sit down next to me.

'How are you?' I asked her.

'I'm good.' She kissed me. 'What about you?'

'A bit tired. And my neck's sore. How did you sleep?'

'Great.'

'Did you do anything else?'

'No, we were both shattered. But I enjoyed the night in his arms.'

'I can smell him on you.'

'He's marked me with his scent.'

'Is he still asleep?'

'Yes. I managed to untangle myself. I wanted to check you were okay.'

This was good to hear. 'I'm fine. So … are you going to tell me?'

'You really want to know what it was like?'

'Yes.'

She looked me straight in the eye. 'I never knew it could be like that.'

'The best you've ever had?'

'Definitely. He's done that a lot of times with a lot of women. He knew exactly what he was doing. And he's got a fantastic body.'

'You seemed to like it.'

'Did you see his muscles?'

'You think he's stronger than me?'

'He is so much bigger and stronger than you. And his cock's bigger than yours. It felt so much better when it was inside me.'

'Watching you take your clothes off was amazing.'

'You've seen me take my clothes off a thousand times. You must be bored by now.'

'I will never get bored of that.'

'I *was* nervous, just at that moment,' she said.

'Why?'

'I didn't know what he'd think.'

'You've got a great body, Tina.'

'I know you think so. But it's more than fifteen years since anyone else has seen it.'

'He liked what he saw.'

She opened her bathrobe and looked down at her tits. 'Yes, the girls still have some life in them.'

'You know what was strange?'

'What's that, babe?'

'When I've imagined you getting fucked by another man—'

'And you've imagined that a lot.'

'Yes, I have. I always imagined you in the missionary

position, at least the first time. It was a bit of a surprise to see you on all fours.'

'Like we keep saying, reality is not like fantasy. Maybe that's his favorite position. And I'm glad he chose it.'

'Why?'

'Because it meant he could get his cock even deeper inside me.' She looked me straight in the eye again and spoke every word very clearly as she said, 'And it felt so fucking good. Do you think he'll want to do it again?'

'Are you kidding?'

'Maybe it was just a one night thing.'

'I saw his face afterwards.'

'How did he look?'

'Like he'd just had the best fuck of his life.'

'That makes two of us.'

'You know something? Part of me thought you wouldn't go through with it.'

'You thought I'd chicken out at the last minute?'

'Even when you were both naked on the bed, I half-expected you to say, "Well, it's all right as a fantasy, but obviously I'm not really going to do it."'

'But I did.'

'Yes, you did.'

'Shall I tell you something?' she said.

'What?'

'I feel like I lost my virginity last night. Everything before was just fooling around, just foreplay. Last night, I finally had real sex for the first time.' I put my finger inside her cunt. It was wetter than I'd ever felt it before.

'Hi,' said a voice behind us. Steve was standing there, wearing my bathrobe. Tina pushed my hand away and jumped up guiltily, pulling the bathrobe around her. She seemed embarrassed that he'd caught us together.

'Hey,' she said.

'Hey.' He nodded at me. 'Morning.'

'Morning,' I mumbled.

'Can I get a shower?' he asked.

'Sure. Let me show you.' She went upstairs, and he followed. I waited on the couch. I thought Tina would show him how to work the shower, then come back so we could carry on talking. When she hadn't returned after ten minutes, I went upstairs. The bathroom door was open. They were in the shower together. Water cascaded over them as they kissed. Tina's eyes were closed. Her face was tilted up to meet his. Steve had his hand on her breast. He was squeezing it gently, working her nipple between his finger and thumb. He moved his head away from hers so he could watch her face as his hand went down her body. The bottom half of our shower cubicle is frosted glass so I couldn't see exactly what was happening inside. My wife and her lover were just a pink blur from the waist down. But Tina's lips parted into an ecstatic smile and even above the sound of the shower I could hear her moan. His fingers had found her cunt. I desperately wanted to see what was happening behind the frosted glass. It was frustrating, like watching censored porn. Tina opened her eyes and reached behind him to switch off the shower. I quickly moved away from the door and went downstairs. Twenty minutes later, they came down. She was still in her bathrobe. He was fully dressed.

'I'd better be going,' he said. 'If I hurry, I can still make my tennis match. See you on Monday.'

'I'll be the one in the low-cut top,' she said.

'Any chance you could wear that gray one?'

'Sure. What do you want me to wear under it?'

'How about nothing?'

'But then, when I lean over your desk, you'll see everything.'

He kissed her on the lips. 'It's been amazing,' he said.

Tina nodded. 'Yes, it has. Thank you.'

He looked over at me. 'Have a good weekend.'

'You too,' I said.

He went out, got into his car and drove off. Tina shut the door behind him.

'How was your shower?' I asked.

'I cleaned every inch of him. We can't have him going out all dirty.'

'Did you … do anything?'

'We spent a long time kissing. It was romantic – kissing with the water raining down us.'

'Did he fuck you?'

She paused. I think she was wondering if she should exaggerate to turn me on. 'No. Sex in the shower is one of those things people talk about. But it's not so easy. There's not enough room. And the floor's too slippery.'

'So you just kissed?'

'Not exactly. Let's just say I'm not as clean as he is.'

'What do you mean?'

She opened up her bathrobe. There were snail trails of Steve's cum all over her tits. 'All the time we were in the shower, he had this huge erection. I had to help him with it.'

'Now I've got a pretty big erection myself. What are you going to do about that?'

She looked at the bulge in my shorts. 'What do you want me to do about it?'

'I want you to tell me about every moment. What were you feeling when you kissed him for the first time? What was it like, running your hands over his body? What were you thinking when you were on all fours, waiting for his cock? What was it like, being in the shower with him? How did it feel when he came over your tits?'

'You want to go over every detail again?'

'Yes.'

'Later. We've got to do the shopping.'

Chapter Four

~

SHOPPING? HOW COULD SHE think about shopping? Could we really just get on with our day as normal? I went upstairs to get dressed. The bedroom smelt faintly of Steve's cologne. The condom wrapped in the tissue was in the wastepaper basket. But my books were on one side of the bed. Hers were on the other side. My clothes were hanging in the closet next to hers. It was still our room.

She had another shower. For some reason, she didn't feel completely clean after the first one. Ten minutes later, she came down the stairs. She was wearing jeans and a sweater – just like she does every Saturday. Anyone seeing us walking round the supermarket would never have guessed what had happened the night before. We looked like any other couple. We got some pasta for lunch. We bought some popcorn in case we wanted to stay in and watch a movie one evening. As we turned into the breakfast cereal aisle, we saw our friend, Louise.

'Tina! Rob!' she said, giving us both a hug.

You wouldn't be hugging us if you knew what we'd done, I thought. You wouldn't come anywhere near us.

'How are you?' she asked.

'We're fine,' said Tina. 'How are you and Nathan?'

She shook her head. 'He's away a lot for work. He only comes home every other weekend.'

'It must be great when he does come home,' said Tina.

'It is. But the pressure's on for everything to be perfect. So we always end up having a fight. And then it's time for him to go.' She shook her head again. 'What have you guys been up to?'

'Nothing really,' said Tina.

'Did you do anything last night?'

'One of my work colleagues came round. It was a chance to get to know him a bit better.'

'That's nice,' said Louise. 'I really should do the same with some of the guys at my office.'

Maybe not exactly the same.

'Well, I'd better go. Lots to do today. Nice seeing you both. Let's get together soon!' She walked off down the aisle.

When we got home, Tina suggested we have a glass of wine. We don't normally drink during the day. But I opened a bottle and we sat down. 'What are your thoughts?' she asked me.

'It looks like we're still the same people.'

'Steve fucked me. He didn't turn me into a vampire.'

'We went to the supermarket. We chatted to a friend. Tomorrow, we'll drive out somewhere for lunch. On Monday, we'll go to work.'

'And your point is …?'

'We have the chance to carry on with our lives as if nothing happened.'

'That's good, isn't it?'

'It's great. But … if we keep doing this, we might not be able to.'

'Or look at it another way … we've shown that doing this doesn't change anything, so we *can* keep doing it. How did you feel, watching me with Steve?'

'It was the most erotic experience of my life, no doubt about that. But …'

'But what?'

'But it was humiliating. I was jealous.'

'I thought jealousy turned you on.'

'It does. But last night, there was no way of controlling it. Even if it had all gotten to be too much, I couldn't have stopped it. I didn't like that.'

'If I'd said stop, he'd have stopped.'

'I'm not sure he'd have stopped if *I'd* said it.'

'He might have thought that was part of the game – you begging him not to do it.'

'So what are *your* thoughts?' I asked her.

'I had great sex with a gorgeous man who couldn't resist me. It certainly wasn't humiliating for me.'

'I'm guessing you want to do it again?'

'You know I do, babe.' She took a sip of wine. 'And … Steve was talking to me while he was getting dressed this morning. He was wondering if we were free next weekend. He'd like to come over for the whole weekend – arriving on Friday, leaving on Sunday.'

'What did you say?'

'I said that would be okay.'

I was definitely not in control of the situation. I was annoyed. I thought we'd been discussing whether or not we should do it again. And now I found out it was already a done deal.

'You're the only one who hasn't cum yet,' she said. 'Shall we go upstairs and put that right?'

Suddenly, I wasn't annoyed anymore.

It took us less than a minute to put it right. Afterwards, Tina lay with her head on my chest. She was soon purring softly. I felt my eyes closing. We slept for an hour. When I woke up, I looked down at her. She was beautiful. I loved her so much. She woke up and looked at me through sleepy eyes. She kissed my chest and said, 'You know what, babe? I think this is going to work. You and I can keep going the way we've always done. Steve can come round every now and then. It won't affect anything else in our lives. And it's very different. He fucks me. You make love to me. He can have my body occasionally. But you'll always have my heart.'

I rolled her gently onto her back. And yes, we made love. We kissed passionately. We held each other. I told her how much I loved her. It was the second time that day, so I even managed to make it last fifteen minutes. It was the best sex we'd had in ages. Maybe Tina was right. Maybe this was going to work.

Chapter Five

~

ON THURSDAY NIGHT, I finally got to see what Tina had bought at Victoria's Secret more than a week ago. She came downstairs in a scarlet bra and panties combination. She wore them with white stockings that were so sheer, they were almost see-through. There were little scarlet bows between her breasts and on the waistband of her panties. 'What does this outfit say?' she asked.

'I'm a present for you to open,' I replied.

'Not too far from the truth.'

She went upstairs. A few minutes later, she came down in a simple white babydoll with white lace trim. 'All sweet and innocent,' I said.

She did a little twirl. 'Isn't it supposed to be every man's dream – a woman who looks like a virgin and acts like a whore?'

Her final outfit was a black lace teddy with plunging neckline and matching black thong. 'So what do you think, babe?'

'You look fantastic in all of them.'

'I've got one more idea.' She went upstairs. A moment later, she came back down. 'I've decided this is what I'll be wearing when he arrives.'

She was naked.

'Not very subtle,' I pointed out.

'There's no need to be subtle now. We don't have to pretend that he's coming round for coffee. How do I look?'

'No man could resist you.'

'Well, *you'll* have to resist, Rob. I'm saving myself for him.' She sat down. 'Let's watch some TV.'

'Aren't you going to put some clothes on?'

'No. You can look but you can't touch.'

She turned on the TV. I found it hard to concentrate on the program.

ON FRIDAY EVENING, I got home first and spent some time cleaning the house. Tina came in at six. She was alone. It was shaping up to be a rerun of the week before. 'Would you believe it?' she said. 'Another crisis at work. He said he'd be here as soon as possible, but he might be held up for a while. I'm starting to think God's against us.'

God's against adultery – who knew?

She went upstairs. I heard her turning on the shower. She came down a few minutes later. She was naked and carrying her bathrobe. The water had turned her nipples into little pink bullets. Her closely cropped dark brown pubes looked fluffy and inviting. She'd spiked up her hair. We wouldn't be seeing the respectable office manager again until Monday. She put a strip of five condoms on the arm of the couch. Even for Steve, five seemed a bit optimistic.

She put her bathrobe over the back of the couch and sat down next to me. I knew I wasn't allowed to touch her, so I didn't try. We heard a car on the street. 'Go and see if that's him,' she said. 'I can't go out dressed like this.'

I went to the door and looked outside. 'Nothing,' I said.

'Why isn't he here?'

'He said he'd be held up for a while,' I reminded her.

'If you knew there was a naked woman waiting for you, would you still be at work?'

'He doesn't know you're naked.'

'Maybe I should send him a photo of myself.'

'That's a really bad idea.'

'It might get him here more quickly.'

'Or it might go viral on the web.'

We talked about work, but we weren't really listening to each other. We sat and waited a long time. When it got to eight o'clock, I started wondering if we should get something to eat. Finally, we heard a car pull up. I opened the door and saw Steve coming up the drive. 'I'm so sorry,' he said. 'I was just packing up when David said some figures had to be sent to Hong Kong tonight or ....'

He stepped inside. I closed the door. Tina launched herself at him. 'Shut up,' she said. 'The last thing I want to think about right now is David.' She undid Steve's belt and roughly pulled down his trousers and shorts. That would shut anyone up. Last time, they'd got off to a slow start. This time, nothing was going to stop Tina from getting exactly what she wanted. Steve looked surprised. You don't expect to have your trousers pulled down by a naked woman the second you step into someone's house. Even his cock seemed a bit surprised. It was only semi-erect. Getting down on her knees, Tina cupped his balls in her hand. She lifted his cock out of the way so she could run the tip of her tongue over his balls. She moaned softly as she felt his cock growing into the hard thick rod she wanted so much. She put her lips around it and sucked gently. As he felt his cock going deeper and deeper into her soft warm mouth, Steve moved his hand around to the back of her head. He took a handful of her hair between his fingers and held her head still. He started moving, fucking her mouth. He looked down at her.

'Is it okay if I ...?' he asked.

She looked up with a mouthful of cock and nodded. She'd never let anyone cum in her mouth. There was a look of triumph on his face. Maybe he sensed that he was about to do something no man had ever done before. This made him cum more quickly than usual. With a long, low groan, he came inside my wife's mouth. She looked up at him and opened her mouth wide. Then she turned to me, her mouth still open. She wanted me to see her mouth full of his cum. Some of it escaped from the corner of her mouth and dripped onto her tits. She closed her mouth and swallowed.

'You get that cock hard again soon,' she told him. 'I want it inside me. But in the meantime ….' She stood up and walked over to me. The last time, I'd faded into the background. She'd concentrated so completely on him that she hadn't paid any attention to me. 'Why don't you fuck me while we're waiting for Steve to get hard again?' She kissed me, pushing her tongue into my mouth. She wanted me to taste his hot, salty cum on her tongue. She bent over the arm of the couch.

It was the first time in my life I'd had sex while someone else watched. I was nervous. It was like playing guitar with Eric Clapton watching. I knew I couldn't be as good as him but I didn't want to embarrass myself. I didn't want to cum immediately and turn round to see Steve smirking. I was already hard and my cock was looking quite big. I turned slightly towards Steve so he could see that I wasn't some cuck with a two inch dick. I put on a condom and pushed my cock into Tina's cunt. I started moving inside her. She moaned. *You see*, I wanted to tell Steve, *you're not the only one who can turn her on*. I would have given anything to fuck her until she came, but I hadn't managed that in all the years I'd known her. I wasn't going to start now. So I concentrated on not cumming too quickly myself.

I tried to think about work and about what I needed to buy next time I was at the store. I tried not to think of Tina sucking Steve's cock. I tried not to think of her showing me her mouth full of his cum. I tried not to think of him standing there, watching me and waiting his turn to—

'Can I cut in?'

I looked round. It had only been a few minutes since Steve had cum, but his cock was already hard. 'I'm almost finished,' I said.

'Let him in, Rob,' said Tina. I pulled out. Steve put on a condom and took my place. If she'd moaned with my cock inside her, she screamed when she felt his. 'That's what I'm talking about!' she said, breathlessly. He fucked her hard and fast. It took him less than a minute to make her cum. I like to think part of that was due to the start I'd given her, but she was probably still turned on after sucking his cock. He pulled out of her, took off the condom, and dropped it on the floor. Then he jerked his cock a couple of times. A rope of his cum flew through the air and landed on Tina's back.

'I'll get a tissue,' I said.

'Tissue?' said Tina. 'You'll need a towel.'

I got a towel from the kitchen and cleaned Tina's back. She stood up and looked at Steve. 'Please tell me you've got another one of those inside you.'

'I'll do my best,' he said.

'You boys play nice,' she said. 'I'm going to make us something for dinner.'

She put on her bathrobe and went out, leaving Steve and me standing there. We both had our trousers and shorts round our ankles. The difference was that he'd cum twice and I hadn't cum at all. We pulled our trousers up and sat down.

'Busy week?' I asked him.

'Yes, quite busy. You?'

'Same. Have you been playing much tennis recently?'

'Not much. Too busy at work.'

'Me too.'

'Shall we watch some TV?'

'Okay.'

I turned on the TV. After half an hour, Tina came back in. She'd made Chinese-style noodles. She sat down on the couch and motioned Steve to sit next to her. I sat on the chair. 'What have I missed, Rob?' she asked.

'There's a man alone in a hotel room. He took a drink from the water bottle in the minibar. Now he's staggering round the room, clutching his throat. I do not ….'

Tina joined in. 'I do not have high hopes for his future.'

Steve looked at us as if he thought we were a bit childish.

After we'd finished eating, Tina sat back on the couch and draped her feet over Steve's knees. That's how she normally sits to watch TV, but it's usually *my* knees. As the evening wore on, her bathrobe got looser and looser, eventually falling open to expose her right breast and more of her well-toned legs. I wasn't surprised that Steve couldn't keep his attention on the TV. At first his hand just rested casually on her knee. Then it started to move up her thigh. She opened her legs slightly, and his hand disappeared under the bathrobe.

'I think I've seen this program before,' he said to Tina.

'Is this the one where someone gets murdered and the team works out who did it?' she said.

'How about an early night?' Steve said with a grin.

'Good idea.' They stood up. Steve went upstairs. Tina stopped and turned to me. 'Do you mind if it's just the two of us this time, babe?'

'That's okay,' I said, quietly.

'You're a good man,' she said. She kissed me on the lips. 'I love you very much.'

I wasn't feeling very much loved at that moment, so I just nodded. She went upstairs. I was better prepared this time, having stashed my pajamas and extra pillows in the den. I was hoping I could make myself more comfortable. I changed into my pajamas and lay down. The arm of the couch I was using for a headrest was the same one my wife had been bent over a couple of hours before. The thought excited me.

My excitement grew as I heard Tina's first moan from upstairs. I tried to imagine what they were doing. Was he using his fingers? Was he licking her? Maybe they'd skipped the foreplay. Maybe they were already having sex. Did he have her on all fours again? Or maybe she was on top. I imagined her sitting on his cock – their pubes meshing together. I thought about the way her tits bounced as she moved up and down. Would he lie back with his hands behind his head and enjoy the view? Or would he reach up and massage her tits with his strong fingers?

I started pulling on my own cock. As the noises from the bedroom grew louder, I jerked off faster. I heard Tina scream and I knew she'd had another shattering orgasm. A second later, I heard Steve's triumphant shout. I wondered where he'd cum. Was he still inside her? Had he pulled out and shot his load over her tits or in her face or …? I came into my hand.

All three of us had cum at about the same time. For a second, I felt like I was part of something that was good for all of us. Tina was the sexiest woman in the world. Steve gave her the great sex she needed and deserved. And all I wanted to do was watch and listen while they screwed.

A second later, I hated the whole situation. I often feel a bit down after I've cum, but never like this. Once again, I wanted it all just to disappear. Steve had done his job. Now it was time for him to leave. Why did he want to stay the whole weekend, anyway? Did he really think Tina could spend two days doing nothing except fucking? She wasn't a machine.

I couldn't find a tissue in the den, so I had to do an awkward, hunched run upstairs to the bathroom. As I came out of the bathroom, I saw the bedroom door was ajar. I looked in. Tina was in Steve's arms. Her eyes were closed and she was naked, a look of complete satisfaction on her face.

I went downstairs and curled up on the couch. I tried to

imagine Tina coming down and saying, 'We've decided that's enough for one weekend. He's going now.' But I knew that wouldn't happen.

Chapter Six

~

THE NEXT MORNING, THEY came down together. Steve had brought a change of clothes and was wearing jeans and a blue shirt. Tina was wearing jeans and a blue sweater. I had no idea what was going to happen. Were we going to go shopping as usual? If we met Louise again, would we introduce her to "our friend Steve, who's staying with us for a couple of days"?

'I stuck my head out the bedroom window,' said Tina. 'It's cold but it's sunny. Why don't we go for a walk in the woods?'

The woods were three miles away. We took Steve's car, and I sat in the back. Tina sat next to him. There were a lot of cars on the patch of ground near the woods. Other people had had the same idea. But there were dozens of different paths going through the woods. I knew we'd soon be alone.

We took our favorite path, which led to a small lake. When we were near the heart of the woods, Tina looked around. No one was in sight, so she slipped her hand into Steve's.

'Look, Rob,' she said. 'There's a rabbit – over there, under the tree.' A few minutes later, she said, 'Is that a deer over there?'

Steve didn't look up. Tina and I loved walking in the woods. But he looked a bit bored. Tina broke away from him and ran up to a tall tree. She hid behind it, then popped her head out from behind the trunk. She put her hands on the hem of her sweater. 'Do you dare me, Steve?' she said.

Steve didn't reply, but he wasn't bored anymore. I looked up and down the path. No one was coming. With a quick movement, Tina pulled off her sweater. She had nothing on underneath. The cold made her nipples stand out. She stood with her back against the tree, her hands behind her. 'Stand at the side of the tree and put your arms around it,' said Steve. It was erotic, watching my wife posing topless among the trees. But there was also a certain innocence about it, like she was a nymph frolicking in the forest.

We heard a noise behind us. We turned round. Two men were coming through the trees on the other side of the path. When they saw Tina, they stopped and stared. Tina looked startled for a second, like a deer surprised while drinking. Her arms instinctively moved to cover her breasts. Then she smiled and let her arms fall by her side. Steve turned and shouted at the men, 'What are you looking at?' He made a move as if to chase them away.

One of them held up his hands. 'It's okay, man; we're just taking a walk.'

'Walk somewhere else,' said Steve. The man looked angry. He didn't like being told what to do. But then he saw how big Steve was. He and his friend walked away and were soon lost in the trees. 'Cover yourself up,' said Steve. Tina put her sweater back on. We didn't say much for the rest of the walk. Steve soon suggested that we turn around and go home.

The atmosphere in the car was strained as we started the drive home. After a few minutes, Tina said, 'How much do you think those guys saw?'

'They saw what you showed them,' said Steve.

'I didn't mind them looking,' she said. 'If you hadn't scared them away, we could have had some fun.'

That would have worked on me. It didn't work on him. 'You

should have covered up as soon as you saw them.'

'I don't have anything to be ashamed of.'

'Don't do that again.'

We drove the rest of the way in silence. When we got home, Tina said she wanted to check her emails. I went into the kitchen to make lunch. Steve sat down in the den to watch TV. I chopped up tomatoes and cucumbers. I put them in a bowl and splashed vinegar and olive oil over them. Tina walked in. 'Any emails?' I asked.

'I didn't look,' she said.

'Trouble in paradise?'

She shut the door and lowered her voice. 'I was angry about what he said in the car.'

'So was I.'

'Telling me what to do.'

'Are you going to talk to him about it?'

'I don't know. We don't want him to leave.'

Part of me would have been quite happy if he'd left. 'Do you want me to talk to him?' I asked.

'No. He probably just said it without thinking. He might not even remember it now. There's no point making a big deal out of it. Shall I set the table?'

She went into the dining room and started laying out the knives and forks. She was just bending over the table when Steve came in from the den. If he was aware that things were tense between him and Tina, he didn't show it. Putting his arms around her waist, he leaned over and kissed her neck. She seemed ready to forgive him. She pushed her ass back into his crotch. He put his hand up her sweater. She straightened up, put her head back against his shoulder, and moaned at the feel of his fingers kneading her tits and tweaking her nipples.

I went into the dining room so I could see them better. She raised her arms above her head so he could take off her sweater. I looked out of the dining room window. I was fairly sure none of the neighbors could see in. Cupping her tits in his hands, he took her right nipple between the finger and thumb of his right hand and twisted it gently. Her eyes were closed. Her mouth was open. She reached behind her to squeeze his bulge through his trousers, moaning in anticipation as she felt what was waiting for her.

She took off her jeans and panties to reveal the perfect curve of her ass. He dropped to his knees to kiss and stroke her buttocks. Then he parted them gently. She gasped. This wasn't what she'd been expecting. His tongue darted into her tight little asshole. The gasps of surprise changed to noises of pure pleasure as the tip of his tongue moved around her hole. When her asshole was moist enough, he pushed his finger in a little way. 'How does that feel?' he asked her.

'It's good, but it's not enough.'

'You want more?'

'Oh yeah.' She turned her head and saw me watching them. 'Rob, could you bring in that bottle of olive oil from the kitchen?' I went into the kitchen and picked up the bottle. I tried to hand it to Tina, but she shook her head. 'I want you to get me ready.'

Steve stood up. I got down on my knees behind her and took the cap off the bottle. I spread her buttocks. I'd licked and fingered her asshole many times. But she'd never let me fuck it. She'd always said, 'Why do you want to fuck that hole when there's a much better hole just next door. Don't you love my pussy?'

Her asshole was already moist from Steve's tongue. I had no trouble putting the tip of my finger in. I poured the oil down my finger. As I continued to lubricate her hole, I was able to push my finger in further. She felt so hot and tight inside – I could imagine how it would feel around my cock. But I wasn't preparing it for me. When I'd finished, she turned to face me. I saw her wicked grin. 'Now get *him* ready.'

'What do you mean?'

'You know what I mean. Come on, Rob.'

'But—'

'Yeah, come on, Rob,' said Steve. 'What are you worried about? I've fucked your wife often enough to show you that I'm straight.'

'Remember, you're doing it for me – if that makes you feel better,' said Tina.

My heart was beating very fast as I poured some oil into my hand. I'd never touched another man's cock before. I took a deep breath and ran my hand up and down his shaft. It felt strong and powerful, like an animal poised for the spring. And it was as hard as a steel bar. It felt like it could drill a hole in the wall. I couldn't imagine what it would do to my wife's sensitive little asshole.

When it was glistening with oil, I put the bottle down. Tina bent over the dining table and reached back to part the cheeks of her ass. 'Help him, Rob,' she said. 'Make sure he finds the right way.' Still on my knees, I took Steve's cock in my hand and placed the tip of it at the entrance to her ass. It was so slippery that I had to hold his cock in position. The head of his cock looked so big next to her asshole. I thought it would never go in. It was like trying to get a fist through the eye of a needle. But he pushed slowly forwards. Then it was like her asshole gave a little gulp and he was inside her.

I sat back to watch. I was thinking my humiliation was complete. My wife had made me prepare another man to do something I longed to do myself.

She was breathing heavily. 'Are you okay?' asked Steve.

'Oh yes,' she said.

'Tell me if it's too much,' he said.

'Just fuck me, you bastard.'

As he moved inside her, he reached around. His fingers found her clitoris. His hand was a blur. The feelings from her clit and her asshole were making her whole body shake. Her gasps of pleasure got closer together until they combined into a squeal of ecstasy. She was feeling things she'd never felt before. The feel of his big cock wedged inside her ass combined with his fingers on her clit was pushing her to a new place. She finally came with a noise I'd never heard in all the time I'd known her. It was a low grunt that emanated from the very heart of her.

After she'd cum, her body went limp. He had his arm around her waist, supporting her, his cock still inside. She hung on him like a rag doll. 'How you doing?' he asked.

She opened her eyes. 'Wow,' was all she could say.

'Do you want to stop?'

'No, you've got to finish too,' she said. 'I'll finally get to feel you shooting your cum into me.'

He took hold of Tina's hips and thrust several more times. He stopped. His buttocks tensed and I knew he was cumming deep inside my wife's ass. He pulled out. 'Can I get a tissue?' he asked me.

I already had a box ready. I handed him one.

Tina was still bent over the table. 'Rob, come and clean me up,' said Tina. She heard me pulling a tissue out of the box. 'Don't use a Kleenex,' she said. I knew what she meant.

Kneeling down behind her, I opened her buttocks with my thumbs. I told myself I was just eating my wife's ass. I'd done it before. I could do it again. I dipped my tongue in tentatively. 'Get right in there, babe,' said Tina. 'Lick it all up and let me see it on your tongue.' I licked up the cum that was oozing out of her asshole and held it on my tongue. She looked round so she could see it. 'Now show it to Steve,' she said. I turned my head so he could see. 'Now swallow it.' I closed my mouth. I tried to imagine I was just eating some warm cream. I opened my mouth to show her that I'd swallowed all of it. 'Well, I need a shower now,' she said. She turned to Steve. 'I'm guessing you do as well. Come on, I'll get you nice and clean before lunch.'

They went upstairs, leaving me sitting on the dining room floor. *Now* my humiliation is complete, I thought. I sat there for a few minutes. Then I went into the kitchen. I had a glass of orange juice to get the taste out of my mouth. I washed my hands and carried on making the lunch. Tina came down a quarter of an hour later and walked into the kitchen. She'd changed into a white t-shirt. A black bra was visible under it.

'Are you okay?' she asked me.

'I'm guessing you and Steve have made up now,' I said.

'Yes, we're friends again,' she agreed. She put her arms around me. 'Thank you for everything you did.'

Chapter Seven

After lunch, Steve went upstairs and came down a minute later with a digital camera. 'Seeing you posing in the woods started me thinking,' he said. 'I want to take a few photos of you.'

'Lucky you had your camera with you,' I said.

'I always carry it with me,' he said, unconvincingly.

'I don't think it's a good idea,' I said.

'You get to see Tina every day.'

'You see her most days.'

'Yes, at work. I want to take a few pictures that give me a bit more than she's allowed to show at the office.'

'What sort of pictures?' asked Tina.

'A series of shots – starting with you fully clothed. Then, in each shot, you take something off, until in the final shot you're naked.'

'I can't see much harm in that,' she said.

I still wasn't sure. 'You really want nude pictures of you out there?'

'They won't be "out there," ' said Steve. 'I'm not posting them on Facebook or anything. You don't know how lucky you are,

Rob. You get to go to bed with this wonderful woman every night.'

'Except when you're here.'

'I just want something to remind me of Tina when we're not together.'

'I don't think we can deny him that, babe,' she said.

I shrugged. 'It's up to you.'

Going over to the window, she closed the drapes and turned to Steve. 'I'm ready for my close-up. How do you want me?'

'Why don't you put your coat on? You've just come in. There's no one at home, so you decide to have a bit of fun on your own.'

'Am I just in from work? Or from the gym? Or from the shops?'

'These are photos for Steve to jerk off to,' I said. 'You don't have to worry about your motivation.'

They both ignored me. 'You've been to the gym,' said Steve. 'The exercise has made you horny.' She put her coat on and stood inside the door. Steve took the first picture. 'Take your coat off. Now bend over and touch your toes. You're doing some stretches after a hard workout.'

'And coincidentally giving you a nice shot of my ass.'

'Now take your t-shirt off and let's have a few pictures of you stroking yourself – enjoying the sensuous feel of your body.'

Standing in front of him in just her black bra and jeans, she ran her hands over her taut stomach and teased her breasts by brushing them lightly. 'Still photos do not do you justice,' he said. 'I've got to make a movie of you some time.'

I *really* didn't like that idea. But Tina just smiled. She was enjoying herself. 'Pull down your bra so we can see your nipples,' he said. The camera clicked again. 'Now play with them.' She closed her eyes and parted her lips slightly as she stroked and squeezed them. 'That's great,' he said. 'Then you suddenly realize that you're being watched. You look over here and see me taking photos of you.' Tina looked straight at the camera with her eyes wide and her mouth open. 'Yes, you're shocked at first but then you decide you like it.' Tina smiled at the camera, a little awkwardly. She was not the world's greatest actress. 'Take your bra off, but cover your tits with your hands. Give the camera a teasing look.' She looked more comfortable doing that. She had plenty of experience in teasing. 'Hold your tits from underneath and offer them to the camera.' He knew exactly what he wanted to see. I could only imagine that he'd been lying in bed every night for the last week, storyboarding the scenario in his head. And I must admit that I was getting excited as I watched my wife being captured in all her sexy glory.

'Take your jeans off.' He took a number of shots of her posing in just her panties. She turned this way and that, letting the camera see her tits from different angles. I found myself wanting to see the photos. But I couldn't tell him I disapproved and then ask him for copies. Tina slid out of her panties without being asked. She stood in front of him, proudly naked. He took several shots of her. He crouched down to get a dramatic shot of this beautiful woman looming over him. He shot her from the front, the back and the side.

Now that he had his nude photos of her, I thought the session was over. But he wasn't finished. 'So you're back from the gym. You're horny. You're naked. What are you going to do?' Tina knew exactly what she was going to do. Her hand moved down and she started rubbing her clit. Her other hand was playing with her tits. She closed her eyes and moaned a little. Either she'd just become a much better actress or she wasn't faking it for the camera.

He put the camera down and took off his clothes. I wasn't surprised to see that his cock was hard. The sight of Tina naked, masturbating for the camera was causing my own cock to strain against the front of my trousers. I assumed that Steve and Tina were going to have sex. It showed what had happened to my state of mind. It had become quite normal for my wife to fuck another man in front of me. But I was surprised when Steve handed me the camera. 'Take some shots of the two of us together.'

I was turned on, but I was still trying to think straight. 'This really isn't a good idea.'

'I think it's a great idea,' said Steve.

'So do I,' said Tina. 'You're outnumbered, babe.'

'It's one thing to take a few nude photos. But if it's the two of you – we're talking hardcore.'

'What's wrong with that?' asked Tina. 'You'll be married to a porn star.'

'That's got to be every guy's fantasy,' said Steve.

That wasn't a fantasy I'd ever had. And I was sure it was one fantasy that should never become reality.

'I want to do this, babe,' said Tina. 'It's just a bit of fun.'

I picked up the camera. Even though he was now the male lead, Steve was still the director. 'You thought you were going to have a lonely evening pleasuring yourself. When you see me, you give me a look of pure lust.' She managed this piece of acting very well. 'And obviously, the first thing you want to do is suck my cock.' She got down on her knees. She took his cock in her right hand and put her lips around the head. 'Now look into the camera,' he said. 'Give it a look that says you know you're a bad girl, but you don't care. You can't get enough of my cock.' Tina was getting more and more into it. With her lips still around his cock, she gave the camera one of her most wicked looks.

He told her to stand up. He stood behind her and reached around so he could tweak her nipple with his left hand while rubbing her clit with his right. 'Now lie down and spread your legs.' He lay down with his head between her legs. He directed me to get the camera right in close so I could get some shots of him licking her cunt. He gently parted her lips and ran his tongue over the hood of her clit. He flicked the tip of his tongue up and down. She moaned quietly.

'Move your tongue from side to side,' I said.

He raised his head slightly and gave me a look. He seemed surprised – maybe even a bit annoyed – that I was giving him advice. But I felt this was one area in which I was an expert. No one had spent more time than me licking Tina's cunt. He lowered his head and started moving his tongue from side to side. The volume of her moans increased. I felt vindicated. He only did this for a few seconds. Then he moved up and kissed her belly button. He kissed his way up her body until he was lying on top of her. He kissed her on the lips. He reached down and found the entrance to her cunt with his finger. He put his cock inside her. 'Make sure you get some great shots of this,' he told me. But it wasn't easy. I had a new respect for the makers of porn films. It was difficult to get those penetration shots. There always seemed to be a leg in the way.

'Now for the money shot,' said Steve.

'Where do you want to cum?' she asked.

'I could cum over your tits. That would make a nice picture.'

'Not the *best* picture, though. If I'm going to be a porn star, I want to do it right.'

He knew what she meant. 'You'd better get back on your knees.' She knelt down. He stood in front of her, but at a slight angle so that I had a clear shot. 'Make sure you get this,' he told me.

'If we don't get it first time, I'm happy to do some retakes,' she said.

He started pulling his cock. Tina watched him. 'Get ready,' he said to me. 'You get ready too,' he told Tina. She closed her eyes and opened her mouth. 'Now!' he said. I pressed the shutter. I captured the moment when his cum landed in a diagonal stripe across Tina's face, covering her nose and her left cheek. Some of it went into her mouth. Some went astray and hit her right eye. Her eyes were still closed, but I knew it was going to sting when she opened them.

I got plenty of photos of my wife's beautiful face, covered

with his cum. He was spent, but he still wanted to make sure he got all the shots he wanted. 'Smile,' he told her. 'Look really happy that you've just had a facial.' She grinned. 'Now lick all round your mouth,' he said. 'Try to get as much of it into your mouth as you can.'

I took a few more photos then put the camera down. Her right eye *was* stinging. She went to the bathroom to bathe it. I offered Steve a tissue. But the only thing he wanted was his camera. He sat down and started reviewing the photos. I went upstairs to see if Tina was all right.

Chapter Eight

WE ATE AT THE dining room table that evening. I'd made roast chicken with mashed potatoes and broccoli. After we finished, I said, 'There's a blueberry pie in the oven.'

Tina cupped her hands over her stomach. 'I'm full for the moment, babe. Can we have it a bit later?'

'It'll be ready in a few minutes.'

'I prefer it cold,' said Steve.

'Let's just sit and talk for a while,' said Tina. She refilled our glasses and turned to Steve. 'Do you ever think this is a bit weird, what we've got going on?'

'Sometimes,' he said. 'What about you? Do you feel guilty?'

'No. I'd feel terrible if I were cheating on Rob. I'd hate sneaking around and lying to him, but this is something we both wanted, so why should I feel guilty? Because I'm Rob's property and I'm letting you trespass? Please. We've moved on from that. I've always enjoyed sex. Why should I only enjoy it with the man I love? Being with you, Steve, has reminded me how much I love having sex with someone for the first time. I like the build-up, the tension when two people want each other but don't know if it's going to happen. I like flirting and teasing.'

'I noticed,' he said.

'And then there's that moment when we both know it *is* going to happen. It's like being at the top of a hill on a roller coaster. That feeling of anticipation just before you plunge into the unknown. I like watching a guy undress for the first time. He looks good with his clothes on, but how's he going to look when he's naked?' She leaned across the table and kissed him. 'No problems with you there.' Then she leaned the other way and kissed me. 'Or you, babe. I adore foreplay, as a man uses his hands, lips and tongue to get me more and more excited. But it's also great when a guy can't resist me. He just throws me down on the bed and fucks me because he can't wait a second longer. It's just a physical thing, of course. I suppose it's a bit like when you guys play tennis. You don't need to have any particular feelings for the person you're playing with.'

'I've had some good matches with people I hate,' said Steve.

'And I think it's possible to have good sex with people you hate. Don't worry, Steve, I don't hate you. But I'm sure we could have great sex even if I did.'

'You think you could have good sex with David?'

She shuddered. 'There are limits. I know people say that women want to be loved and cherished while men just want to get laid. And don't get me wrong, I do want to be loved and cherished. And I'm so grateful to Rob for everything he does for me.'

'No problem,' I said, quietly.

'But I also want to get laid. And … don't take this the wrong way, babe ….'

'What?'

'I do sometimes wonder if it's possible to have really great sex with someone you love. I mean, when we make love, Rob, it's wonderful. You make me feel really cared for. But it's not the wild animalistic sex I have with Steve. I know sex is supposed to be all about love. But for me, it's more about that moment when you think: I don't care who you are; you turn me on and I've got to have you. It's like you have no choice. That's how I felt about you, Steve. I watched you in the office and I had to have you.'

'I felt the same.'

She extended her hands, palms out, in a broad gesture. 'Do you see? It was lust – pure and simple. Well, not very pure. But the relationship you have with the person you love is complicated. When Rob gets sick, I look after him. I sponge his forehead and feed him chicken soup. I don't mind doing it because I love him. But I'm basically being his mother. And it's not easy to go from being a guy's mother to being his sex goddess. Love and sex are two different things. Even the language we use is completely different. Sometimes I call you a bastard during sex. Does that offend you?'

'No, I like it,' said Steve.

She smiled. 'Obviously I don't really think you're a bastard. I wouldn't let you in the house if I did. It's just something that pops out occasionally. And sometimes guys have called me a slut and a whore. I'd hate it if they did that any other time. But it turns me on if they say it in bed. Rob never calls me that because he loves me. You can't call someone a dirty whore one minute and a sweet woolly baa lamb the next.'

'Is that what he calls you?' Steve asked, with a certain degree of sympathy in his voice.

'It makes it easier for me,' I said. 'Knowing it's just a physical thing between you guys. In some ways, the hardest thing is watching you two kiss.'

Tina put her hand behind Steve's head and pulled him towards her, kissing him on the lips. He parted his lips and she pushed the tip of her tongue into his mouth. Then she sat back in her seat. 'How did that make you feel?' she asked me.

I didn't hesitate. 'Jealous.'

'That makes you more jealous than seeing him fuck me?'

'I think so. In a way, I've gotten used to seeing you fucking. Like you say, sex is just a physical thing. A kiss is different. A kiss is more about romance.'

'So you'd rather we didn't kiss?' asked Tina.

'It might be better that way.'

'You'd better see to your blueberry pie, babe.'

I went into the kitchen and took the pie out of the oven. I heard Tina talking in a low voice, but I couldn't make out what she was saying. I came back into the dining room with the pie.

'Leave it on the table to cool,' said Tina. 'Let's go upstairs for a while.'

We went up to the bedroom. I took up my position sitting against the wall at the side of the bed. I could feel immediately that something was different. The atmosphere in the room wasn't that of two people who couldn't wait to fuck each other. There was no urgency as Tina undressed herself, quietly slipping out of her clothes and lying down on the bed. Steve was just as calm as he took off his clothes.

He got onto the bed and lay on top of her. They kissed – a long, lingering kiss. He pulled his lips away and brushed the hair away from her forehead. He kissed her shoulder. She tilted her head to one side so he could kiss her neck with quick, fleeting touches of his lips. He moved down her body and kissed her breasts. 'So beautiful,' he said.

His cock slid easily into her. Before, he'd always thrust into her hard, wanting her to feel his size and power. This time they took a moment to be still and enjoy the feeling of togetherness. She looked into his eyes. She raised her head off the pillow so she could kiss him. He started to move slowly. As he moved, he kissed her lips, her eyelids, her neck, her armpits, her breasts.

The blood was humming in my ears as I realized what was happening.

He carried on moving inside her. He had such control that he knew he could make her cum quickly or slowly. He kept up a gentle, steady rhythm until she arched her back off the bed. They looked deep into each other's eyes as she came. She didn't cum with a scream the way she usually did with him. Her orgasm was like a sigh – gentle but intense.

'Did you cum at the same time?' she asked him. He nodded. 'I felt your cum as much as I felt mine,' she said. He pulled out of her and went to the bathroom to clean up. She turned to me with a grin. 'Did you enjoy that, babe?'

'What?'

'I know jealousy turns you on. So tell me you enjoyed it.'

I couldn't say anything.

'Let's go and have some blueberry pie,' she said.

My head was spinning. I needed a drink. Downstairs I opened a bottle of brandy and poured us each a glass and handed out slices of blueberry pie. We sat down again at the table. 'This is lovely, babe,' said Tina.

'Good pie,' agreed Steve. He turned to Tina. 'Have you ever cheated on Rob before?'

Could we please talk about something else? I thought, though I didn't say it out loud. The brandy was calming me down, but my emotions were still churning. Tina didn't answer immediately. She swirled the brandy around in her glass. I was afraid she was going to admit to something I knew nothing about. And I really couldn't take any more that evening.

Finally she said, 'I don't count this as cheating. This is sharing. So I would say I've still never cheated on Rob.' My heart rate slowed down a bit. 'But I haven't always been a good girl. I had this boyfriend a couple of years before I met Rob. He was called Nick. He had real trust issues. He was always quizzing me. "What have you been doing? Where did you go? Who did you see?" If I even mentioned talking to another guy, Nick would say, "Does he know about me? Did you tell him you've got a boyfriend?" I managed to get away one evening and go out with my friend, Carla. We had a few drinks and then we went to get a burger. At the burger joint, we started chatting to these two guys. One of them was called Kieran.'

I thought I'd heard all of Tina's stories, but this was new to me. I'd heard about Nick, of course. But Kieran? Who was he?

'He wasn't what you'd call handsome but he was an interesting looking guy. He had long dark hair and very pale skin. He was dressed all in black. Vampire chic. He and his friend were nice guys and they made us laugh. They said they were students. Their place was just around the corner. They asked us if we wanted to go and eat our burgers there.

'It was a small apartment. Considering two guys lived there, it was quite tidy. They opened a bottle of wine. We sat around the kitchen table. They told a few jokes. It was good fun. Carla was into Kieran's friend. I can't remember his name. They went off to his room. Kieran asked me if I wanted to see his room. I couldn't imagine there was much to see, but I said yes. We sat on his bed and kissed. He didn't ask me if I had a boyfriend. I must admit the thought of Nick made me enjoy kissing Kieran even more. Nick would have gone crazy if he'd known I was even eating a burger with another guy. And here I was with Kieran's tongue in my mouth.

'Kieran put his hand under my sweater. That's when I had to tell him the bad news. I'd got my period that morning. I knew he was disappointed. But he made the best of the situation and asked, "Can I fuck your tits?" I stood up and took off my sweater and my bra. I also took off my trousers. The poor guy wasn't going to see my pussy. The least I could do was show him my legs. His bed was bolted to the wall and too narrow for him to straddle me comfortably. So I lay down on the floor. He didn't take his shirt off. He just pulled off his jeans and his shorts. When I saw his cock, I was cursing the menstrual gods. He had the most beautiful cock I've ever seen. It was huge.' She looked at Steve. 'It was even bigger than yours. I've always wondered what it would have been like to feel that cock inside me. He had big balls as well. I wanted to feel those balls bumping up against my ass as he screwed me. But it wasn't to be.

'I offered to spit on my tits for him. But he said he'd fuck them dry. He stood with his legs on either side of my hips and lowered himself down. I wrapped my tits around his cock and held them in position as he started to move. I was so turned on …. I lifted my head so I could see his cock between my tits. It didn't last very long. After a while, he got up and stood over me. He stroked his cock a couple of times and came all over me. Those big balls had a lot of cum in them. Most of it went on my tits but he got some of it on my legs.

'He gave me a Kleenex. Then we put our clothes on and went back into the kitchen. We had another glass of wine and chatted while we waited for Carla to come out of the other guy's room. It was some time before she did, so I guess Kieran's friend was quite impressive.

'When she finally appeared, we headed off. We didn't make any plans to meet again, but as we were leaving Kieran said, "You know where to find us." I asked Carla how she'd got on. She said it had been good, but she didn't think she'd be going back for more. I told her she was a slut. She laughed and said, "You can't talk. You stink of cum. You'd better hope Nick's not waiting for you when you get home." I hadn't thought about that, but it was the sort of thing he did sometimes.

'I was in a bit of a panic when I got back to my place. Fortunately he wasn't there. I jumped into the shower and destroyed the evidence. After that, I always had a quiet smile when Nick complained because I'd said hello to some guy in the street. If he'd only known ….' She took a sip of brandy. 'That's the only time I've been unfaithful to anyone. Once in thirty-six years. That's a pretty clean rap sheet.'

She put her elbows on the table and looked at Steve. 'How surprised were you when we went to that bar and I asked you if you wanted to do … all this?'

'I knew you were interested in me. Sometimes when I was in the office, I could feel your eyes on me.'

She rolled her eyes. 'And I thought I was being so subtle.'

'But I assumed it was just one of those office things. Flirting that wasn't going anywhere. So, yes, I was quite surprised when you suggested … all this.'

'It didn't bother you that she was married?' I asked him.

'It made it more of a surprise, but it didn't really worry me. My folks aren't religious, so I never had it drummed into me that God punishes adulterers.'

'Have you ever been with a married woman before?' asked Tina.

He paused for a moment, as if wondering how much he should reveal. Then he nodded. 'Yes, I have.'

'Was she beautiful?'

'What?'

'I want to know if she was beautiful. I've just made Rob more jealous than he's ever been in his life. It might do me good to get a taste of my own medicine. Come on, Steve, make me jealous.'

'She wasn't as beautiful as you.'

'Liar,' she said, with a smile. 'I bet she was a hundred times more beautiful than me.'

He hesitated. He didn't know the rules of this new game. 'Well, yes,' he began, 'I suppose some people might say she was more beautiful than you.'

'Sexier too?'

'Yes, she was much sexier than you.'

'And every time you're with me, you're thinking about her?'

He was watching her face carefully, trying to gauge her reaction. 'It's all I can do not to shout out her name,' he said.

She smiled encouragingly. 'What was her name?'

'Hailey.'

'I'll remember that. So where did you meet Hailey?'

'At a friend's barbecue. I noticed this woman sitting on her own, so I went up to her. I asked her if she was there alone but she said no, she was with her husband. He'd spent the whole evening chatting with his friends and hadn't said a word to her since they'd arrived. I started talking to her. We got on well. But then her husband saw me. That made him pay her some attention. He came over and said they had to go home. I thought I'd never see her again. But a couple of days later, she phoned me. She needed some excuse for calling and I'd told her that I go down the gym a lot. She said she was having trouble toning her arms and could I help her. I didn't believe that any more than she did, but you've got to play along. I was able to get her a one day free trial at my gym.

'We arranged to meet there one evening. We played around with a couple of weights for a while. Then I walked her back to her car. The gym parking lot wasn't very well lit. There had been complaints from members but I was quite happy about it at that moment. I asked her if there was anything else she wanted, apart from help toning her arms. She said her husband wasn't interested in her anymore. She said she didn't want to leave him. She wasn't even looking for an affair. She just wanted to feel attractive again. Then she asked me, "Am I attractive?"

'I kissed her and told her she was very attractive and that her husband must be a jerk for neglecting her. She had changed out of her sweats into a short skirt. I put my hand up her skirt. I just brushed her cunt through her panties and she almost screamed. It was a long time since she'd been touched. I grabbed her panties and gave them a sharp pull. They ripped easily. I put two fingers inside her. She was so wet, she could have fucked a beer can.

'I pushed her down on the back seat of her car and got on top of her. My cock slid into her with no resistance at all. She undid the buttons of her blouse. She was wearing a frilly white bra. "My husband bought me this bra," she said, "but he's never seen me in it. I want you to rip it." I took her bra in both hands and pulled it until it ripped.

'I fucked her hard and fast. I knew that was what she needed. I fucked her until she came. Then I pulled out. I asked her where she wanted it. She pulled up her blouse. I came over her belly. I wasn't sure what I was supposed to do next. I didn't know if part of her fantasy was that I just got up and walked away afterwards.

'I got out of the car. She put out her hand so I could help her up. She buttoned up her blouse. "I'm going home with no panties and no bra," she said. "And you know what? He won't even notice." She handed me the remains of her bra, telling me I could keep it as a souvenir. She straightened herself up, then got into the front seat and drove off.

'I never saw her again. I was glad about that, to be honest. She was only doing it to take revenge on her husband. I didn't want to get in the middle of that. But I didn't feel bad about fucking her. It wasn't like I was breaking up a happy marriage.'

'And what were her tits like?' asked Tina.

'They were ... nice,' said Steve, still unsure what to say.

'Nicer than mine?'

'I guess so.'

'And did they turn you on?'

'I was quite turned on by the whole situation. You know, doing it in the back of her car ....'

'Are you saying her tits were nicer than mine?'

'I don't know if they were nicer—'

'Are you saying her tits were nicer than mine?'

'Yes, they were nicer than yours.'

'And was she prettier than me?'

'You're not even in her league,' said Steve.

'What would you do if she phoned you right now?'

'I'd be out the door.'

'You'd pass up sex with me for the chance of sex with her.'

'In a second.'

'Do you want to go to bed now?'

'Yes.'

She took him by the hand. 'Goodnight, Rob,' she said, as she led him up the stairs. 'You stay here.'

I didn't move from the table. I'd watched my wife making

love with another man. It was the most painful, and at the same time, most intensely exciting experience I'd ever had. I told myself Tina had only done it to turn me on. I was aware for the first time that somewhere in the world was a man called Kieran. I didn't know anything about him except that he'd once cum all over my wife. I poured myself another brandy and tried to imagine what was happening in the bedroom. I listened. I could hear their voices but couldn't make out the words.

Then I heard Steve call out, 'Oh, Hailey, you're still the best!'

Chapter Nine

~

AFTER A FEW MINUTES, I heard the bedroom door open. Tina came softly down the stairs in her bathrobe. 'He's gone to sleep. Can I sit with you for a while, babe?'

'Of course you can.' We went into the den and sat on the couch. I put my arm round her and pulled her towards me. She rested her head on my chest. She smelt of Steve, a scent I was getting used to.

'Did I go too far tonight?' she asked.

'We're playing with strong emotions here.'

'I know. But you said you were getting bored of just watching Steve fucking me.'

'No, I didn't. I said maybe I was getting used to it.'

'Even so. I thought maybe it was time to up the stakes a bit.'

'You knew the one thing that would make me even more jealous would be watching you and Steve making love.'

'And it worked.'

'Does Steve know why you did it?'

'Yes.'

'So you told him it was just to make me jealous?'

She paused. 'Well, no. I just told him I wanted to make love.

But coming after the conversation we'd just had, he must have known. He's not stupid.'

'Are you sure about that?'

'Don't be nasty, Rob.'

'And why were you quizzing him about that Hailey woman? You've never said anything like that before.'

'No, I haven't.' She thought for a moment. 'I guess I just wanted to see what it was like. Maybe I was trying to understand you a bit better. You obviously get off on knowing that Steve is better in bed than you. I wanted to know what it was like to be compared to someone else. So, when we were in bed, I got Steve to tell me about Hailey again. I made him recount all the details about what she looked like and what they did in the back of her car. And I made him tell me that she was the prettiest, the sexiest, the best.'

'And did you enjoy it?'

'Yes and no. I've decided it's not really my thing, but it did make me very competitive. I was determined to prove that I'm better than Hailey. So I used all my tricks. I used my hands, my mouth, and my tits to stimulate his cock. I laid him down and rode him.

'And don't worry; we definitely didn't make love this time. I called him a dirty bastard. He called me his cheap little fuck-toy and said I was a total skank compared to Hailey. But after we'd cum, I made him admit that I was the best ever, a hundred times better than Hailey. The poor guy got very confused about what he was supposed to say. But he did get to cum inside me, so let's not feel too sorry for him.'

'Do you want me to start talking about my ex when we're in bed together?'

'What, tell me that Deborah was so much hotter than me?'

'If you like.'

She kissed me. 'No, babe. I'm the best you've ever had. You're the worst I've ever had. And that's the way we like it.'

'Okay,' I said.

'Do you still love me?'

'Of course I do.'

'Well, you enjoy your night on the couch, babe. I'm going up to spend the night naked in bed with another man. I don't love him. But I'm madly in love with his cock.' She felt my bulge through my trousers again. She smiled when she felt how hard I was. 'You're a strange man, Rob Matthews,' she said and went upstairs to bed.

As I got ready for another night on the couch, I started thinking. Why was I so turned on by the thought of my wife being in love with another man's cock? I could imagine an analyst delving into my childhood to look for answers, but I didn't think he'd find much there. My parents had a normal, stable marriage. As far as I know, there was no infidelity on either side. They loved me and my sister very much. There was only one thing from my childhood that might have influenced my thinking.

My father was a philosophy professor at the local college. He believed in moral relativism. From when I was a small boy, he told me that very few things are absolutely right or absolutely wrong. I was taught that an action is right if it makes people happy and wrong if it makes people unhappy. And generally it seemed that the situation Steve, Tina, and I had created was making people happy. Steve was happy. He got to have great sex with a beautiful woman. Tina was happy. She had the security of a loving marriage. But she was free to have wild sex with Steve.

My feelings were a bit more complex. Sometimes I wanted Tina all to myself again. There were times when I resented Steve's presence in our house. But there was no denying that I loved watching them together. My lust for Tina was never stronger than when I saw her giving herself totally to another man. And I loved talking to her about it. But that brought me back to the question of why.

I think I can trace it back to experiences I had when I was at college. Although I've got some confidence in my looks now, I didn't when I was a teenager. I had very bad skin. This made me shy and reluctant to leave the house. I spent a lot of time alone in my room, listening to Morrissey. I had some female friends, but none of them were interested in being anything more than that. I got used to hearing lines like: 'I love you as a friend' or 'You're more like a brother to me.'

I was still a virgin when I went off to college. During my first year there, I met Deborah. I first saw her in the college bar, watching a football game on the big screen. She was matching the men beer for beer and trash-talking the other team's fans. She was acting like one of the guys. But she was also very feminine – large green eyes, auburn hair that flowed down to the small of her back. She had large breasts that bounced around inside her sweater every time she jumped up to celebrate. And she drew attention to them by saying things like, 'If I keep doing that, I'll have two black eyes.'

I didn't much like her that first time I saw her. I thought she was too loud. Five minutes with her would give anyone a headache. But a couple of weeks later, while I was having lunch in the crowded cafeteria, Deborah asked if she could share my table. We started talking and I saw a different side to her. She liked reading and music. She even liked a lot of the same authors and singers I did. She also loved sports. I've never been a sports fan but I nodded at her comments and pretended to know more than I did.

We talked for most of the afternoon. We both missed a couple of classes. She asked me if I wanted to go back to her room. Experience had taught me not to get my hopes up. Back then, if a girl invited me to her room, it was usually because she wanted a sympathetic ear while she complained about her boyfriend. We walked to the house she shared with two guys and three girls. She made me wait in the kitchen while she went upstairs to tidy her room. I didn't care about the state of her room, but she insisted.

Ten minutes later she called down the stairs. She was waiting at the door of her room. She let me in and shut the door. She didn't say anything. She just kissed me and put my hand on her breast. That's when I knew it was finally going to happen. I was actually going to have sex. I had to stop myself from getting too excited. I'd heard stories about what happens to male virgins their first time. At least I hadn't ejaculated spontaneously when I first touched a breast. I was proud of myself for that.

We sat down on the bed and kissed. She could tell I was nervous. 'Don't worry,' she said, 'I've done this loads of times before.' I know this is the last thing most men want to hear, but I was relieved. One of us had to know what we were doing. She unbuttoned her shirt. She wasn't wearing a bra, and her boobs came tumbling out. I tried not to focus on them.

I took a long time over the foreplay. I knew the actual sex wasn't going to take very long. I thought if I gave her as much pleasure as possible with the foreplay, it would increase my chances of being asked back to do this again. I stroked her hair, kissed her neck, and ran my hands gently over her body. If I couldn't be a great lover, I could at least get the consolation prize of being a sensitive lover.

Her little moans told me I was doing the right thing. 'Take your clothes off,' she said, 'including your socks.' She reached under her bed for a packet of condoms and handed me one. My fingers were shaking as I opened the packet. Then there was some nervous fumbling as I tried to put the condom on inside out. Fortunately, she just laughed. 'You're so cute,' she said.

When I finally had it on the right way, I lay down on top of her. I felt the entrance to her cunt with my finger and tried to get the tip of my cock into the same place. But I couldn't find it. She reached down and took my cock in her hand. Putting it in the right place, she said, 'Now try.' I pushed and felt my cock slide into her. I'd also survived the first experience of a girl touching my cock. But being inside a woman was the biggest test.

I tried to do some math in my head. What's sixty-five multiplied by twenty-seven? Well, five times seven is thirty-five. So that's five, carry the three ….

'Are you okay?' she asked. 'You look like you're in pain.' I guess I always screw my face up when I'm trying to do math.

'I'm just enjoying it so much,' I said.

'Okay, Rob, go for it,' she said. I started moving inside her. By trying to work out a hundred and forty-nine divided by eight, I managed ten reasonable thrusts before I came.

As I felt my cum pumping into the condom, I thought, This is it. I'm actually cumming inside a woman. It didn't last very long, so it's possible she'll never want to see me again. But, whatever else happens, I'm not a virgin anymore.

Afterwards, I lay with my head on her chest. I was so grateful to her, I felt like crying. I'd happily have bought her a new car if she'd asked. Fortunately the only thing she asked was, 'So how many lucky ladies have enjoyed the Rob Matthews treatment?'

I was glad to hear her ask this. It meant she hadn't realized it was my first time. I thought of admitting the truth, but I was afraid she might laugh. And if she got a few beers inside her, she might share it with her friends. I didn't want everyone in the bar singing 'Like a Virgin' the next time I walked in. On the other hand, I didn't think she'd believe me if I claimed to be a super stud with hundreds of notches on my bedpost. 'Five,' I said.

'Including me?'

'Including you.'

'You're still a bit of a slut,' she said with a grin.

From virgin to slut in one day. That felt good. 'What about you?' I asked.

'Three.'

'Only three?'

'You thought I'd been out whoring all over town?'

'It's just that you said you'd done it loads of times.'

'I have, but mostly with the same person. My last boyfriend

was a bit of an animal. He couldn't keep his hands off me.'

My cock twitched when she said that. And I think that was where it all started – the beginning of my fetish for hearing about women with other men.

'What was he like?' I asked.

'He was a bit older – he was quite experienced,' she said. I interpreted that as: he was better than you.

I was a bit surprised to see my cock was hard. 'Would you like to go again?' I asked.

She also looked surprised. 'Aren't I the lucky girl today?' She lay back.

The second time, I spent even longer on the foreplay and managed to last twice as long when I was inside her. When I'd finished, I slid beneath the sheets. I kissed my way down her body until I reached her cunt. I really had no idea what I was doing down there. I went at it with the clumsy enthusiasm of a dog at his water bowl. But she was happy to be my teacher. 'Use the tip of your tongue. This is a precision operation. The broad brush approach doesn't work. The clitoris is important, but don't focus on it all the time. Spend some time on the area around it. Up and down. Now side to side. Now round and round.'

After twenty minutes of hit and miss, I made her cum. When it was over, I sat up. Trying to sound as casual as possible, I asked her, 'So, what are we doing here?'

'Oh, I thought you knew,' she said. 'It's called sex. It's what people do when there's nothing on TV.'

'You know what I mean. Are you my girlfriend now?'

She paused for a second. I knew what she was thinking. She was wondering what her friends would say if she walked into the bar holding hands with me. 'Do you want me to be?'

'Yes.'

'I should warn you, you'd be taking on a lot. I'm very moody. I've got quite a temper, as well.'

A few sullen silences and the occasional raised voice seemed a small price to pay for regular sex. 'No problem,' I said.

'Okay, then. Why not?' It wasn't a passionate declaration of love. Juliet on the subject of Romeo would have put it better. But it was good enough for me. It meant I was in a sexual relationship with a woman. But, as we started going around together, it turned out to be more than that. I had someone to do things with. If we were feeling cultured, we went to a museum or a concert. If we weren't, we just had a few drinks in the college bar.

People *were* surprised when they saw us together. I'm sure they expected her to be with some jock who played football every afternoon and drank ten beers every evening. And they probably expected me to be with the president of the chess club. I saw more football games than I wanted to and drank more beer than I'd ever done before. I went to a lot of parties and stayed up late more times than I should have done.

And yes, she was moody. There were some days when I couldn't get two words out of her. And she did have a bit of a temper. Sometimes she yelled at me for no reason. But it wasn't long before she apologized. And then we had make-up sex.

We had a good time together. We made each other laugh. And we spent a lot of time in bed during the day. It's one of those things you can do when you're at college.

One afternoon, we were in bed, just waking up from a post-coital doze. She asked me, 'Am I the best sex you've ever had?'

I was about to say, 'Well, seeing as you're the *only* one I've ever had, there's not much competition.' But I remembered that she was supposed to be my fifth. 'Oh yes, definitely.'

There was a silence when she should have said, 'You're the best I've ever had too.' But she didn't.

'You're definitely the best,' I told her again, just to make it clear. She still didn't reply. I should have let it go, but something made me ask her, 'So, am I the best you've ever had?'

'You're very caring,' she said. 'You make me feel loved.'

'But?'

'But, like I told you, my last boyfriend was a bit older, a bit more experienced.'

'So he was better than me?'

'Well ... yes.'

'What did he do?'

'Do you really want to know?'

'Maybe I can get some pointers.'

She got out of bed and took a photo album from the bottom of her wardrobe. 'Let me show you some pictures of him,' she said, as she got back into bed.

I was sitting up in bed next to my naked girlfriend, poring over pictures of another man. There was a picture of the two of them on a beach somewhere. Fit and tanned in a white swimsuit, she had her arm around the waist of a tall man with sun-bleached hair. He had his arm around her shoulder.

'He's called Josh,' she said. 'He's gorgeous, isn't he?'

'I'm not a great connoisseur of male beauty,' I mumbled.

'I know, but you must admit he's a good-looking guy.'

'I suppose so.'

She turned the pages of the album. There was a photo of her in a stunning scarlet dress standing next to Josh, looking very suave in a tuxedo. There was another photo of them in a restaurant with a group of friends. She had her head resting on his shoulder.

Suddenly she kissed me passionately. It was the kiss she always gave me when she wanted to have sex. She put the photo album on the floor by the bed. She lay back with her eyes closed. I started kissing and stroking her. Then I noticed the way she was smiling. It was a nostalgic smile. She was thinking about the past – about Josh.

It made me jealous. Why did she need to think about someone else when she was in bed with me? But I was also turned on. When I got inside her, I came almost immediately, but I didn't make a big thing about it. I gently pulled out and replaced my cock with my fingers. The feel of my fingers moving inside her, coupled with the images of her ex running through her head, were enough to bring her to orgasm.

She opened her eyes and she was back with me again. She put the photo album away and we didn't say any more about it. I had an assignment to write, so I went back to my own room. I wasn't sure what had happened. I was a bit worried that I'd been so turned on. As a young man, I constantly asked myself the question, 'Am I normal?' This suggested I was anything but normal. But, I told myself, it was just a one-time thing. I didn't want Deborah thinking about Josh when I was in bed with her. So I promised myself I would never mention it again.

But being turned on is a bit like being drunk. It can make bad ideas look like very good ones. The next time we were in bed, I couldn't help asking, 'So ... how ... you know ... *big* was Josh?'

'What?' she said. She looked a bit shocked.

I tried backpedaling a bit. 'I was just wondering. But if you don't want to tell me, that's fine.'

'Why do you want to know?' Before I could say anything, she answered her own question. 'Does it turn you on?'

'A bit,' I said.

'Okay, if you must know, roll over and I'll show you.' I rolled onto my back. She held her finger about an inch and a half above the tip of my erect cock. 'It was about this big.'

'So it was bigger than mine?'

'Yes, it was bigger.'

I rolled her onto her back and fucked her, hard and fast. She soon realized that, if she ever wanted to have sex, she had a button she could press. All she had to do was mention Josh and I was ready.

After that, we nearly always talked about him in bed. Occasionally she said, 'Can't it just be the two of us sometimes?' And I would promise not to talk about him next time. But then I would find it difficult to get aroused and she would say, 'Josh never had any trouble in that area.' And suddenly I was hard.

Looking back, I can see that a lot of what excites me now came out of my experiences with Deborah.

I was still with her when I met Tina. It was a cold, sunny morning. Tina was standing outside the main campus building. She looked very pretty in a short black jacket and a black beret. She was handing out flyers for someone called Joseph P Weaver, who was running for student president. I took one of them.

'What does your candidate stand for?' were the first words I ever said to her.

'I have no idea,' she said. 'One of my friends just asked me to hand these out. I haven't even read them. He might be a neo-Nazi for all I know. Do you want to help me?'

I didn't like the idea of distributing neo-Nazi propaganda, but I knew I wanted to spend some time with her. I took a quick look at one of the flyers. His main policy was to improve street lighting on campus. I had no ideological issues with that, so I could hand out the flyers with a clear conscience. I even started saying things like, 'Vote for Joseph P Weaver! Get the representation you deserve!'

'You're a natural,' said Tina. When we'd rid ourselves of all the flyers, she said, 'Thanks. Can I buy you a cup of coffee?'

I did wonder what Deborah would say if she saw me with another woman, but I wasn't going to say no. We went to the coffee shop and started talking.

There was something different about her. With Deborah, I always had to pretend a little bit. I had to convince her that I was a bit louder, a bit sportier, a bit more of a party person than I actually was. With Tina, I could be myself. I assumed we were just going to be friends. After all, she was far too pretty for me. A woman like her should have been dating some guy with a chiseled jaw and a trust fund. I kept waiting for her to throw in a reference to her boyfriend on the gymnastics team or the guy back home she was engaged to. But she didn't.

We kept running into each other. We drank a lot of coffee.

We talked a lot. And one afternoon, she leaned forward and kissed me on the lips. I kissed her back. I didn't know if this was going to be our one and only kiss, so I made sure I enjoyed it. Then my conscience made me pull back. 'Isn't this what you want?' she asked.

'Yes, I do. Very much. But I'm with Deborah.'

'So why do you spend most of your time with me?'

I went up to Deborah's room. She could tell from my expression that I had bad news for her. 'Deborah,' I began, 'you're wonderful ....'

'But you're breaking up with me. I've been wonderful three times in my life before and every time I've had my heart broken.'

'Heart broken?'

'You're a nice guy, Rob. A bit weird maybe, but a nice guy. I could kind of see myself ending up with you.'

'Sorry.'

'It's Tina, isn't it?'

'That obvious?'

' "Tina said the funniest thing today," and "I'm reading this great book that Tina lent me." Do you want to have sex one last time?'

'Better not.'

'You see, that's a nice guy. Most men jump at the chance of break-up sex. Well, you go and find Tina. I hope you'll be happy.'

'Thank you.'

'Do you mind if I give you some advice?'

'Please do.'

'It's probably not a good idea to quiz Tina about her ex-boyfriends when you're in bed together. She might think it's odd.'

I knew this was excellent advice. And the first few times I was with Tina, I didn't need anything more than her naked in bed. She did ask me, 'What do you like?'

But I answered with bland things like, 'Sexy underwear. The girl going on top.'

Then one night, after I'd been with her for three weeks, we were in her room together. We kissed. I undressed her. I was kissing her breasts when I started to worry. I couldn't feel my cock straining impatiently. I reached down and felt it. It was soft and limp.

'What's the matter with you?' I asked my cock – internally, of course. 'We're in bed with the most beautiful woman we've ever seen. She is very keen to have sex. And you're not in the mood? Come on! This is your job!'

But my cock did not respond well to being bullied. If anything, it retreated into itself and got even smaller.

'What's wrong?' asked Tina.

'Don't worry. Just a slight technical problem.'

She looked down and saw what I meant. 'We'll have to see what we can do about that,' she said. 'What would turn you on most right now?'

'Just being with you is a huge turn-on. I don't know what's the matter with it.'

'I've been having a rather naughty fantasy. Would you like to hear it?'

'Oh yes!'

'Well, we're on a train, in a crowded compartment.' I wanted her to say that she fucked everyone else in the compartment in front of me. 'And we are just so horny. So I get up and go off to the bathroom.'

Please say there's some handsome stud waiting for you in the bathroom.

'And a few seconds later, you follow me. You join me in the bathroom and lock the door behind you.'

Darn it. It was a fantasy about me.

'I'm wearing a short skirt. I pull it up and take off my panties. I bend over the basin. And your cock is *so* hard. It's like rock. You just get it out and push it into me from behind. The feel of my pussy and the movement of the train go together to give you the most incredible orgasm you've ever had. Do you like that fantasy, Rob?'

'Yes, I do.' I liked the fantasy very much. I was even wondering when we could take a train trip together.

'But *he* doesn't,' she said, looking down at my cock. 'What does he need?'

'Well,' I began, tentatively, 'there is one thing that might work.'

'What?'

'I'm guessing I'm not the first guy you've ever been with.'

'You're not one of these men who's obsessed with a finding a virgin, are you?'

'No, just the opposite.'

'I don't understand.'

'How many guys have you had?'

'Why do you want to know?'

'I just do.'

'Eight.'

'And what did you do with them?'

'What do you mean?'

'When you were in bed with them, what did you do?'

'Er ... we had sex.'

'What sort of sex?'

'I don't know what you want me to say. It was just sex.'

'Was it better than what you have with me?'

'Look, Rob, I'm not sure what's going on here. But I don't feel comfortable talking about my ex-boyfriends. They're people I cared about.'

'Sorry.'

'Is this your thing? Hearing about me with other guys?'

'It's sometimes worked in the past.'

'I might be able to help. I mean, you're not the first who's been around here today. Dirk was here earlier.'

'Dirk?'

'He came round and fucked me. He's got a twelve-inch cock.'
'That's pretty big!'

'And he fucked me ten times – one after another without stopping. He made me cum about twenty times.' Tina's fantasizing skills were still a bit raw in those days. She hadn't realized yet that plausibility is an essential ingredient in a great fantasy. But it was enough to make my cock hard.

'You're strange,' she said, as she lay back on the bed and I got on top of her.

ON SUNDAY MORNING, I woke up at half past eight, got up and made breakfast. I didn't really have a hangover, but I could feel that I'd been drinking the night before. I moved a little bit more slowly round the kitchen. I made pancakes and ground some coffee beans. I hoped the smell of real coffee would drift upstairs and make Tina and Steve come down.

Ten minutes later they did come down. They didn't show any signs of suffering from the brandy the night before. They both looked fresh. But they weren't saying much to each other. Tina turned on the TV and we watched it as we ate breakfast.

After we'd finished, Steve went upstairs to get his bag. 'Well, I'd better get going,' he said, when he came back down. He kissed Tina. 'You were amazing,' he said.

'You didn't do so badly yourself,' she replied.

'Thanks for breakfast,' was all he said to me.

'No problem.' He left. Tina closed the door behind him.

'Everything okay?' I asked her.

'Sure. Why?'

'You were both a bit quiet this morning.'

'We were together all day yesterday.'

'So, is he coming again next weekend?' I asked.

'No.'

'A weekend on our own for once?'

'I'm afraid not, babe. He asked me to go over to his place.'

'What?'

'He says it's unfair, expecting us to be the hosts all the time.'

'Did he invite me, as well?'

'No. He also said he'd like a weekend where it's just me and him.'

'And did you tell him that's not the way it works?'

'No, I kind of said it would be okay.'

'What? The whole point is—'

'I'll tell you all about it when I get back. Just imagine how great that will be.'

I tried to focus on that. And I was glad to have Tina to myself for the rest of the day. We did the shopping for the week. We made calls to family. We cleaned the house. At the end of the day, we sat down on the couch to eat dinner. Her legs were back where they belonged – draped over my knees. We didn't talk about Steve or anything that had happened. We needed to spend some time just being us.

At ten o'clock, we went to bed. I put my arm around her and we went to sleep.

Chapter Ten

~

ON TUESDAY EVENING, TINA was quiet at dinner.
'How was your day?' I asked her.

'Fine.'

'Any problems with David today?'

'No.'

I couldn't remember the last time she'd gone a whole day without any David issues. 'You okay?'

'Yes.'

She didn't want to talk so I didn't press her any further. After dinner, she said she was tired and wanted to go to bed. I decided I might as well get an early night too.

When I went into the bedroom, Tina was in bed under the quilt. She pushed the quilt away. She was naked. 'So, Rob,' she said, 'do you want to have sex?' It sounded like a simple question. But her lips were pursed. Her eyes were hard. Even so, I took my clothes off and got into bed with her. 'And I suppose you want me to talk about Steve?'

'If you want to.'

'Well, let me tell you something about Steve. When I'm in bed with him, I don't have to think about what I'm going to say next. I can just relax and enjoy it. I'm enough for him. He doesn't need to imagine me with someone else. Do you think *you* could try that some time, Rob? So, are you ready to have sex?'

Needless to say, I was definitely not ready to have sex. She gave my limp cock a look of contempt. 'Oh, just go to sleep.'

She turned over. I got out of bed, put on my pajamas and turned off the light. When I got back into bed, I didn't try to touch her or put my arm around her. I lay there, staring into the darkness. For years I'd been asking her to tell me all these stories like she was my own private sex line. And all she wanted to do was lie back and enjoy it. Maybe that was what she really liked about Steve. Maybe it wasn't the way he looked, or his cock, or his technique. Maybe it was that she could just enjoy the moment.

When I woke up next morning, Tina was already out of bed and getting dressed. 'Hey,' she said with a smile, when she saw me open my eyes. She seemed to have forgotten all about it. So I let it go.

ON SATURDAY MORNING, I woke up with Tina lying on top of me. Her head was on my chest, and her left leg was between my legs. I could feel something damp on my thighs. I lifted up the sheet. My legs looked like something out of a splatter movie.

Tina woke up and immediately knew what had happened. She groaned. 'I've got my period,' she said. 'I wasn't expecting it for another couple of days. The weekend with Steve isn't going to happen.'

I started planning what we could do. I thought we'd do the shopping. We might go for a walk. I even wondered if I could book a table at our favorite restaurant. It was usually quite busy on a Saturday night, but you never know, they might have a cancellation.

We got out of bed and went to the bathroom to clean up. 'I'd better give him a ring and tell him,' she said. She went off to call him while I went downstairs and made some coffee. Five minutes later, she came into the kitchen. 'He's picking me up in an hour.'

'He still wants you to go 'round?'

'That's what he said.'

'So what are you going to do, talk about the weather?'

The anger I'd seen on Tuesday flashed back into her eyes. 'I suppose it never occurred to you that he might actually enjoy my company.'

'But the whole idea—'

'Yes, the whole idea is that everyone does what you want so you've got something to jerk off to.'

She went to get dressed. I made breakfast. We ate in silence. Then she went upstairs to pack her bag. I followed her up and stood in the doorway of our bedroom. 'I'm sorry,' I said.

She nodded and said, 'I'm sorry too. I shouldn't have reacted like that.' I noticed she was putting several sets of sexy underwear into the bag. They weren't going to spend all weekend talking about the weather. 'Sometimes I think this is getting too complicated,' she said.

'We can stop any time.'

'I know. We'll talk about it when I get back tomorrow evening.'

'You don't have to go if you don't want to.'

'I do. I promised him.' She managed something close to her wicked smile and said, 'And, anyway, I do want to. Shall I tell you something before I go? You love my tits, don't you?'

'Yes.'

'How much do you love them?'

'They're the most beautiful things I've ever seen.'

'Well, they're not *my* tits this weekend. They're *his*. I'm going to give them to him as a present. He can do whatever he wants with them. He can touch them and kiss them. I'm going to let him put his cock between them and fuck them. I'm going to let him cum all over them. Are you hard?'

'Yes.'

'Do you want me to make you cum before I go?'

'Yes.'

We heard Steve's car outside. 'Sorry, I've got to go,' she said. She looked down at my hard cock. 'I'll leave you two alone. See you tomorrow. Be good, because I won't.'

She gave me a quick hug and went downstairs. I heard the front door slam. I went to the window and watched her getting into Steve's car. They drove away. I was left in the house alone.

I tried to convince myself that this was great. It was a night in on my own. I had no one to please except myself. I could do all the things that Tina didn't like. I could order some Mexican food. I could watch a James Bond movie. Or I could call up some people I hadn't seen for a while. Ever since I'd been with Tina, my social life had revolved around her. I'd neglected my friends. There were a couple of guys I knew from high school. They only lived a mile or so away, but I hadn't seen them in years. We could go out for a few beers.

The only problem was that I didn't want to. I wanted to eat pizza and drink wine with Tina. I didn't want to see anyone else. I didn't want a few beers. I didn't want to eat Mexican food. I certainly didn't want to watch a James Bond movie. He could have sex with anyone he wanted and there were no consequences. Well, sometimes the girl got blown up afterwards, but there were no consequences for Bond. He just put his tuxedo back on and got on with the mission. My life wasn't like that. Sex had consequences for me. And the consequence now was being alone in the house and wishing my wife was here with me.

When it got to nine o'clock that evening, I decided to call her. There couldn't be any harm in phoning just to say good night. She might tell me a few details about what they'd been doing during the day. That would make me feel like I was part of it. At the very least, I'd get to hear her voice. But when I called her number, I just heard an anonymous, robotic voice saying, 'The person you are calling is not available. Please leave your message after the tone.'

'Hi… it's only me,' I said. 'Just calling to … say hi. Okay, hi. Well … bye.'

Even as I was saying it, I knew how pathetic it sounded. I went to bed. The bed without Tina in it was even colder than the couch.

Chapter Eleven

~

ON SUNDAY, I TIDIED the house then went to the store and bought pasta. I put a bottle of Tina's favorite white wine in the fridge. I cleared the dining room table and put a clean tablecloth on it. I even got out the candles. I lit them when I heard the car outside at around seven. Tina came in. 'What's the occasion?' she asked, when she saw the dining room.

'You coming home.'

She sat down at the table and I poured her a glass of wine. 'How was your weekend?' she asked me.

'I spent most of it working,' I lied. 'I caught up with a lot of boring admin. What about yours?'

'It was good. He's got a very nice apartment. There's no way he could afford it on the money he gets working for us. And when he talked about the holidays he took as a kid, it didn't sound like he came from a rich family. But maybe there's a wealthy aunt in the background somewhere. The ground floor is all one big room with a kitchenette at one end. And there's this marvelous fireplace in gray stone. An old metal spiral staircase runs up the middle of it, leading to his bedroom and the bathroom. It's a real bachelor's apartment. There are no doors except on the bathroom. Wherever you are in the apartment, you can see everywhere else.'

I really didn't need this much detail. I wasn't planning on buying the place. 'So, what did you do when you got there?' I asked.

'He made some coffee, and we sat on the couch. We talked about the company ball. David's going to make a speech. I wondered if it would be possible to tie hooks to David's pants so they ripped off when he started talking.' She paused to savor the image, a crafty little smile on her face. 'David's asked Steve to speak, as well. He's got to run through the annual figures. I don't think he's looking forward to it. How do you make annual figures interesting?'

I leaned forward. 'And then what happened?'

'He cooked this fantastic dinner. I had no idea he could cook. He never said anything about it. But it was real Cordon Bleu stuff. We started with a dozen oysters, which he showed me how to eat. He served those with champagne. Then he cooked a beef stroganoff with beautiful sautéed potatoes and garlic asparagus.'

I looked down at the plate of pasta I'd made for her. Suddenly, it looked rather basic.

She carried on. 'We had a pinot noir with the main course. As you can imagine, we were quite full after that, so we had to wait half an hour before dessert. He'd made a *panna cotta* flavored with marsala wine. Then after dinner, we sat in front of the fire and shared a glass of Cointreau.'

'Champagne, red wine, and Cointreau. How drunk were you?'

'I was fine. When I woke up this morning, it took me a couple of seconds to work out where I was. I was alone in a strange bed. Then I heard his footsteps coming up the staircase. He'd made breakfast – freshly squeezed orange juice, bacon, and waffles. He got back into bed and we ate it together.'

'But you got there at about ten in the morning yesterday. You must have done something between then and dinner.'

'We watched some TV.'

'Is that all you did?'

She sighed. 'You want to hear about the sex, don't you? Well, we couldn't go all the way, but we fooled around.'

'Fooled around?'

'Can't you use your imagination?'

'I've been using my imagination all weekend.'

She sighed again. 'Okay. He had this magazine on the coffee table. It was about cars, but it had a woman in a bikini on the front cover. I asked him if he found her attractive. He said she was okay. I told him her boobs were fake. She'd definitely had a job. Then I took his hand and put it up my shirt. I said, "These aren't fake, are they?" He squeezed them and shook his head. I unbuttoned my shirt so he could have a better look.'

'What were you wearing underneath?'

'A bra.'

'Which one?'

'I can't remember. For me, a bra is just something to stop my boobs from bouncing around. It's not the center of my universe. Do you want me to carry on?'

'Yes.'

'Of course you do. Well, he nibbled my nipples through the bra. He took me by the hand and led me up the staircase to his bedroom. He asked if he could Kieran me.'

'Kieran you?'

'He remembered me talking about that guy Kieran who fucked my tits.'

'Oh yeah. What happened next?'

'I took my bra off and lay down on the bed. He put his cock between my tits.'

'And then what did he do?'

'What do you think he did? He fucked them.'

'Did he cum?'

'Of course he did.'

'Where?'

'Some of it went in my hair. Some went on the pillow. Most of it ran down my neck.'

'Did any go on your tits?'

'I don't know. Probably. Next time, I'll get the crime scene guys in to analyze the spatter pattern.'

I ignored her sarcasm. 'And how did you feel?'

She shrugged. 'Like someone had just cum on me.'

'Did you tell him they were his tits for the weekend – your present to him?'

'Yes. It sounded a bit lame when I said it to him, but he liked it. And he said something to me …'

'What?'

'I'm not sure I should tell you.'

I swallowed. 'You've told me everything else. How bad can it be?'

'Just before he came, he said he loved me.'

I felt my jaw go slack. 'What?'

'He said, "I love you, Tina." '

'What did you say to that?'

'I said, "I love you too". But don't worry. It's just the sort of thing you say when you're in bed with someone.'

Heat rose in my cheeks. 'No, it isn't. What were you saying the other day? There's the language of sex and there's the language of romance. "I love you too" is definitely the language of romance.'

'Well … I only said it turn you on.'

'I wasn't there!'

'I knew you were going to ask me about it later.'

'And did he know that?'

'I'm sure he did.'

I had to ask, though I dreaded her answer: 'Tina, are you starting to have feelings for him?'

She made a face. 'No. Of course not. Don't be silly, Rob.'

I shook my head. 'I think we need to ease off a bit.'

'Maybe. But not now.'

'Why not?'

'It wouldn't be fair on him to go from "I love you too" to "We're finished" just like that.'

'But he knows you only said "I love you" to turn me on. Remember? And I'm not saying you should finish with him. Just cool it down. Maybe just see him every other weekend.'

She shrugged. 'Okay, I'll talk to him.'

We sat down to eat the pasta. I thought it best not to ask her any more about the weekend. So we talked about our next vacation. We wondered if it might be possible to visit both Paris and Amsterdam in one trip. It felt good to be making plans with her. Talking about the future was reassuring. We went to bed early. I put my arm around her. I felt the warmth of her in the bed again, but I couldn't sleep. I had a lot of things going through my head.

When she came home from work on Thursday, Tina said, 'I don't know if you'll be interested, but that time of the month isn't that time anymore.'

We went upstairs, took off our clothes, and got into bed. For tonight at least, Tina was all mine. I imagined Steve sitting on his own, dreaming about her. But then I told myself to put Steve out of my mind. Just her and me.

'Get that cock hard,' Tina said. 'I need it inside me now.' It was good to hear about her desire for *my* cock. That was enough to get me hard. But it took too long to open the condom packet and I lost my erection. 'Do you want me to talk about Steve?' she asked.

Part of me knew this was a bad idea. But her tone sounded seductive, rather than exasperated, as if she actually wanted to talk about him. 'Yes,' I said.

'Because I never told you about Sunday morning, did I? After he'd cooked that delicious breakfast, I wanted to do something for him. You know, to say thank you. I stood in front of him in just my panties.'

'What color?'

'What?'

'What color were your panties.'

'Black, I think.'

'Did he look at your tits?'

'Of course he did. I think he loves them even more than you do.'

'That's not possible. Then what did you do?'

'He was wearing these silk boxer shorts in bed. They were sexy. You should get a pair. Anyway, I got back into bed and slipped under the covers. I pulled down his boxers and got his cock out.'

'Was it still bigger than mine?'

I heard that sigh again. 'Well, it didn't shrink in the wash. Sorry. Yes, it was still much bigger than yours. But I don't think I've ever told you how much I love the taste of it. I've tasted a few cocks in my time. But none of them taste as good as his.'

'Does it taste better than mine?'

'So much better than yours, babe.'

'Did you make him cum?'

'Of course I did.'

'Where did he cum?'

'I lay on my back and said, "Here's my body – shoot your load anywhere you want!"'

'Where did he pick?'

She sighed again. 'He came all over my stomach.'

'And how did that make you feel?'

I should have picked up on her sighs. But I didn't. So I was shocked when she suddenly yelled, 'How do you think I felt? Honestly, Rob, you're never satisfied, are you? You're like some guy at a strip club going, "Give me more! Give me some more!"'

'Sorry.'

'Yes, you're always sorry. But the next time you're back to, "And then what did he do? And what did you do? And did he see your tits? And did you suck his cock?" I feel like I'm just 3D porn to you. And you know what, Rob? I'm sick of it.'

She stood up and left the room. I heard her going downstairs. She didn't want me to follow her, so I didn't. I stayed in bed. I heard her speaking on the phone. Then I heard her going into the cupboard under the stairs. She came up the stairs and back into the bedroom. She put the big suitcase onto the bed. She opened drawers and started pulling out her clothes. She stuffed them into the suitcase.

'What are you doing?' I asked.

'He's picking me up in ten minutes.'

'What?'

'Right now I feel like he's the one who loves me for me. I'm going to try living with him for a while.'

I felt the life drain out of me. 'But, Tina ….'

'I'm sorry it's come to this, Rob. But I don't know … maybe you're pleased.'

'Why would I be pleased?'

'Because this is all your fantasies come true. You're obsessed with the idea of me in bed with another man. Now it's going to happen every night. It's your ultimate wet dream.'

'But I love you.'

She stopped packing. Her face softened a little. 'I love you too. I really do, Rob. But I can't carry on like this. I feel like a slut going from one man to another.'

'But you said—'

'Yes, I know what I said. Something can sound like a smart philosophy of life after a few glasses of wine. It's not so easy when you try to live it. I'm your wife, for heaven's sake. A real husband would want to beat up the guy who was screwing me. He wouldn't just sit there jerking off about it. And yes, I know we talked about it. I know what we agreed. But right now, I need a guy who just wants me. And that's not you.' We heard a car pulling up outside. 'Stay there, babe,' she said. She came round to my side of the bed and kissed me. 'I'll call you tomorrow.'

She went downstairs. The door closed behind her. I heard her getting into Steve's car. The car drove off. I was still in bed, naked. I have never felt more alone – or more stupid.

Chapter Twelve

❧

ON MONDAY, I WOKE up in an empty bed. I went into the bathroom. I'd spent the weekend alone. I hadn't showered or shaved for two days. I took a shower but couldn't be bothered to shave. I figured if anyone asked, I'd say I was growing a beard. I made coffee but skipped breakfast. If I felt hungry, there were always cookies in the teachers' lounge.

When I arrived at work, I found Danielle in the teachers' lounge. 'How was your weekend?' she asked.

'Fine.'

She picked up on my tone of voice. 'It wasn't fine.'

'No, you're right. Very far from fine.' I wasn't sure I knew her well enough to share the intimate details of my life, but I didn't have anyone else to talk to. 'My wife left me.'

She walked across the room and hugged me. I was surprised. We'd shaken hands when we'd first met, but we hadn't touched in any way since then. I took a moment to enjoy the feel of being in a woman's arms again. Then I broke away. I didn't want any of our colleagues to see us.

'If you want to talk about it, just tell me,' she said.

'Are you free for dinner tonight?'

She smiled. 'Yes. See you later.' She went off to her first lesson.

I still had half an hour before my lesson so I sat down to think about what I was doing. I'd asked her out without thinking. Part of it was that I didn't want to spend another evening in the house, eating alone in front of the TV. It would be nice to go out to a restaurant. And I'd always liked Danielle. I could spend some time with her and get to know her better. But was there more to it than that? Was I looking for revenge?

Then I remembered what Tina had told me – that I'm an over-thinker. I told myself to relax and just enjoy an evening out with a friend. Danielle probably had a boyfriend back in France. And even if she didn't, she was a beautiful woman. She could do so much better than a married man.

I paid extra attention in all my lessons. I had no safety net now, and if anything happened to my job, I wouldn't be able to cope. Living in a single-income household was going to be hard enough. Living in a zero-income household would be impossible. I'd have to move back in with my mother. And that's a little embarrassing when you're thirty-seven.

After work, I went home and had another shower. I shaved carefully. At the back of the bathroom cabinet, there was an unopened bottle of aftershave lotion someone had given me for Christmas. I splashed some of it on my cheeks. I went upstairs and looked through the clothes in the wardrobe. I didn't want to wear a suit, but equally I didn't want to show up in jeans and a t-shirt. I wondered if there was anywhere I could buy flowers on my way to the restaurant.

I never thought I'd be doing this again. I remembered that, when I first started seeing Tina, I cleaned my college room to military standards. I always put on clean shorts and clean socks and made sure all my best clothes were freshly laundered. I didn't do that for Tina anymore. I came home from work and changed into an old pair of sweatpants. If Tina ever came back, I'd make more of an effort.

Thinking about Tina made we want to phone Danielle and

cancel, but I told myself that wouldn't be fair. I combed my hair one last time. And I left the house – a thirty-seven-year-old married man going out on a first date.

I'd booked us into a little Italian restaurant in a part of town where Tina never went. Danielle arrived on time, wearing the same clothes she'd worn for work. She wasn't dressing to impress.

She kissed me on both cheeks and sat down. 'Let's take some wine,' she said. 'I've had a long day.'

We ordered a bottle of Valpolicella. We spent most of the evening talking about Tina. I told her Tina was having an affair with a work colleague, which made it sound like I was the innocent victim. Danielle made sympathetic noises. Several times she reached across the table and touched my arm. But I couldn't imagine that I was saying anything she'd find attractive. I felt like I was talking as her friend – worse, her whiny friend.

I also found out more about her. She did have a boyfriend back in France. 'When you are going to be apart for many months, you are supposed to say, "I will wait for you!" like in the movies. But he just said, "We'll see how we feel when you come home." We haven't even written since three months.' She gave a broad, Gallic shrug. 'It is not the romance of the century. It would be okay if I had some fun in this country.'

She smiled at me. At that point, I was fairly sure she saw me as more than just a whiny friend. 'Will you walk me home?' she said, after we'd split the bill.

If ever there was a time for over-thinking, this was it. I should have thought long and hard about what I was going to do. It was not a simple tit for tat. Tina had taken things further than I'd ever intended. But we had discussed it. I had agreed that she could have sex with Steve. We'd never talked about me having sex with another woman. I was on the point of doing something that could wreck my marriage. But then again, I thought there was a real chance my marriage was already wrecked. And I had the choice between a night in a cold bed and a night in the arms of a beautiful woman. 'Of course I will,' I said.

It took ten minutes to walk to Danielle's apartment. She put her arm through mine as we walked. 'Shall I give you the grand tour?' she said, when we arrived. 'It will take only a moment.'

The apartment was very small. One room doubled as her living room and bedroom. There were two doors leading off from the main room. One was a tiny kitchen. The other was an even smaller bathroom. There was a collage of photos on the wall above her bed. She saw me looking at it. She pointed to each photo in turn. 'My best friend, Sylvie. My brother, Laurent.' The last photo was of an elegant, dark-haired woman in her fifties standing next to a white-haired man whose face was brown and wrinkled from years in the sun. '*Maman et papa*,' she said. 'My mom and dad.'

'You didn't need to tell me that,' I said. 'You've got your mom's face.'

'You think *maman* is beautiful?'

'Yes, she is.'

'You must think I am beautiful also.'

There was silence. We looked at each other. If I'd kissed her, she would have kissed me back. 'Would you like a drink?' she asked. I nodded. 'Have you ever tried Ricard?' She poured us two glasses of golden liquid. 'And now a magic trick,' she said. She had a small bottle of water on the table. She put just a few drops of water in each glass. The clear gold turned a cloudy yellow. 'Cheers!' she said.

'What do you say in France when you drink?

'*Santé, bonheur, et sexe à toutes heures*! Do you understand?'

'Health, happiness, and sex all the time?'

'Exactly.'

I drank a little. A warming taste of aniseed filled my mouth. She took a sip from her glass. Then she put her glass down, stepped forward and kissed me on the lips. It wasn't like kissing

Tina. Her mouth was a different shape. She didn't move her lips the way Tina did. Her breath smelt of aniseed. Tina hated licorice so she would never drink Ricard.

I told myself not to think about Tina. Danielle was a beautiful, sexy woman in her own right. She didn't deserve to be compared with someone else.

She laid me down on the bed and pulled down my jeans and my shorts. My cock lay there limply. It was feeling guilty. I told it we had no reason to feel guilty. I told it to look at Danielle. She had long black hair, Mediterranean olive skin and deep-brown eyes.

She looked disappointed that my cock wasn't more excited. 'He hates me,' she said. She bent down. Her hair brushed against my thighs as she took my cock into her mouth. She alternated between running her tongue along the shaft and letting the tip flick round the head of my cock. But it still wasn't responding. The photo of her mom and dad looking down at us did not help.

I closed my eyes. Thoughts of Tina filled my head. I remembered the first time I saw Tina sucking Steve's cock. He came to my house. My wife put his cock into her mouth. She sucked it until he came. Then she swallowed every drop. Thinking about this made me hard.

Danielle reached into a drawer and pulled out a pack of condoms. She took one out of the pack and rolled it over my cock. She reached up inside her skirt. With a swift movement she pulled off her panties and tossed them onto the bed. They were red with a white *fleur-de-lis* pattern. They were nice – sexy, even – but they weren't the sort Tina would ever wear.

Still wearing her skirt, Danielle got back onto the bed. She straddled my hips and lowered herself towards me. My cock was inside the tent of her skirt. She reached in, took hold of my cock and maneuvered it into her. Her cunt was hot and tight. It was the first time I'd been inside a cunt that I'd never seen. I hadn't even seen her tits. I reached up and undid the buttons of her blouse. She wasn't wearing a bra. Her tits were smaller than Tina's. Her nipples were chestnut brown.

She pulled her skirt up so that she could rub her clit while she was moving up and down on my cock. I craned my neck so I could see. She didn't trim the way Tina did. She had thick, black pubes. She moved her clit round in rapid little circles. Tina always just rubbed hers from side to side.

I started thinking about the first time I watched Tina masturbate. It was a couple of weeks after we'd got together. We were in bed. She gave me one of her wicked looks and said, 'Do you want to watch me get myself off?'

'Of course I do,' I replied.

'There's no "of course" about it. Some men hate it. It's supposed to remind you that I have a sexuality that's totally independent of you.'

'I want to be reminded of that.'

Tina sat up in bed, propped up by pillows. She started rubbing her clit hard and fast with the fingers of her right hand. She used her left hand to stroke her tits. It wasn't long before she was throwing her head back and gasping as she had a very satisfying orgasm.

The memory of this was too much for me. I felt myself starting to cum. Danielle deserved my full attention – at least while I was cumming inside her. It wasn't a very hard cum. I didn't think she'd felt it pumping into the condom. Maybe I could pretend it hadn't happened.

'Why don't you lie down?' I said.

'What's wrong?' she asked.

'Nothing. I've just got to lick that beautiful cunt.'

'I love that word,' said Danielle. 'Cunt.' It sounded good in a French accent.

She lay down on her back and pulled up her skirt. I kissed her thighs. Her skin smelt different than Tina's. I told myself that I *must* stop thinking about Tina. I had to live in the moment. I got down between her legs and found her swollen clit, buried in thick pubes. I licked it. It tasted good. I was finally able to forget about Tina as I focused on giving this woman pleasure. I pushed my tongue inside her as far as it would go. Her juices were hot and sweet. I moved my tongue quickly over her clit. As her moans got louder, I moved my tongue faster. I tried to imitate with my tongue the circular motion of her fingers. She let out a long deep moan. Her body bucked.

She reached down, took my head gently between her hands and pushed it away. 'Thank you,' she said. I felt a mixture of pride and guilt. On the one hand, I shouldn't have been with Danielle at all. But, on the other, I'd proved to myself that I could still give a woman pleasure.

'Now you,' she said.

'You don't have to do anything,' I replied. 'When I make a woman cum, I feel it as much as she does.'

That didn't sound convincing, even to me, but she nodded. Afterwards, we lay in each other's arms. Part of me wanted to phone Tina and brag about what I'd just done. But a bigger part of me wanted to make sure Tina never found out about it.

'You are guilty,' said Danielle.

'What do you mean?'

'You are thinking about your wife.'

'How do you know?'

'A woman always knows.'

'Sorry.'

'I want you to know you must not worry. When I see you tomorrow morning, I'll just say, "Hi, how are you?" like nothing happened. I won't make any trouble for you and your wife.'

'Thank you.'

'Do you want to stay here?'

'Is that okay?'

'Sure. Do we know each other well enough to use the same toothbrush?'

'I think so.'

We got ready for bed and then curled up together. I put my

arm around her. Danielle was taller than Tina. There was a lot more of her in the bed. Her hair was longer than Tina's. Whatever I did, some of it was in my face. Eventually, we fell asleep.

Chapter Thirteen

~

THERE WASN'T MUCH AWKWARDNESS the next morning. When the alarm went off, Danielle got out of bed and went into the bathroom. Ten minutes later, she came out with a towel wrapped around her body and another around her head. She dressed in front of me. She had a beautiful body. I knew I'd never see it again. 'Do you want to take a shower?' she asked.

'No, it's okay. I'd better go home and get a change of clothes.'

She went into the kitchen while I got out of bed and dressed. She came back with two cups of espresso. We sat on her bed and sipped it. 'I enjoyed last night,' she said.

'So did I.'

'But you are still in love with your wife.'

'Yes.'

'You will be with her again soon.'

'You think so?'

'She's the one for you.'

'I wish she knew that.'

'She does. A woman always knows.' She smiled. ' "When I make a woman cum, I feel it as much as she does." '

'You noticed that, did you?' She nodded. 'I hope you meet the one for you soon.'

We hugged and I went home. I was thinking that the one night stand had ended as painlessly as these things ever did. But that night, I couldn't sleep. There's a line in an Avril Lavigne song where she shouts, 'What the hell were you thinking?' I had that line going round my head. What the hell were you thinking – having sex with Danielle? She's supposed to be your friend. She's here alone in a foreign country. You should be helping her, not fucking her. Is this how you treat your friends – you use them to get back at your wife? And on the subject of your wife, what the hell were you thinking, encouraging her to have sex with someone else? What did you think was going to happen? You thought she'd have sex with another man and then everything would be exactly the same. You'd just have something hot to talk about in bed. But this is reality. These are real people with real emotions. You encouraged her to go after the hottest guy in her office. You let them try out their relationship in your bed. Then, as time went on, you knew she was starting to have feelings for him. It's not like she didn't give you fair warning. But you were so convinced she was in love with you that you didn't do anything. She was falling for the man who was giving her great sex. Why the hell would she come back? What's so great about you? And now here you are, alone in the house.

And that's another thing, what are you going to do about the house? Are you going to buy Tina out? On a teacher's salary? You really think that's going to happen? You'll have to sell the house and move into a tiny bachelor apartment. And we all know what happens to men who live on their own. Dinner will be a ready meal washed down with a bottle of cheap whiskey. You'll crawl into bed at two in the morning after seven hours of mindless channel surfing. The den will be a mess of dirty plates, empty cans and old pizza boxes. You won't leave the house at all during the weekend. You won't wash or shave or change your clothes. The neighborhood kids will start talking about the weird guy who lives by himself. They'll stand outside your door shouting names at you until you chase them down the street in your vest.

And then, one day, you'll open your mail box. For once, there will be a letter that isn't an advertisement. It'll be an invitation to Steve and Tina's wedding. So you'll drag your crumpled old suit out of the wardrobe. And you'll go along. You'll stand there and smile. Tina will come down the aisle. She'll be more beautiful than ever. Steve's going to be next to her, looking like something out of a menswear catalog. She's going to take a quick look at you and think, 'I dodged a bullet there.' She'll be lost forever. You might see her driving by one day with her husband beside her and their adorable children in the back. And all this just because you thought it would be a turn-on to watch her with another man. *What the hell were you thinking?*

Eventually, I must have fallen asleep. The next thing I knew, my alarm was going off. I got out of bed with a new resolve. I was not going to let myself go. So I made myself a proper breakfast. I washed the dishes. I showered and shaved. I went to work.

I decided to get into better shape. Tina wasn't the most health-conscious person in the world. She put in her time at the gym, but she also liked sitting down with a twelve-inch pizza. And she usually just rolled her eyes if I suggested she might like a salad with it.

On my way back from work, I went to the store and filled my trolley at the fruit and vegetable aisle. I bought brown rice, beans, bananas, kiwi fruit. There were a lot of things I hadn't eaten for years because Tina didn't like them.

As I was leaving the store, I saw Tina's gym on the other side of the road. On a whim, I went in. 'I'd like to join the gym, please,' I said to the receptionist.

'No problem,' she said. 'Could I have your name, please?'

'Robert Matthews.'

She typed something into her computer and frowned. 'Robert Patrick Matthews?'

'That's me.'

'You're already a member, sir.'

'Are you sure?'

She turned her computer screen around to show me my name and address. 'You've been a member for the last three years.'

'But I haven't paid anything.'

'Our records show you've been paying every month. The price was reduced because you have joint membership with your wife.'

I had no memory of joining the gym at the same time Tina joined, but I nodded. 'Oh yes. I remember.'

I STARTED GOING FOUR times a week. I lifted weights. Gradually, my arms became thicker. My legs became more defined. Shoulder and chest muscles started to emerge. At the end of every workout, I spent half an hour on the stationary bike or the cross trainer. I also did some crunches on the Swiss ball. If I tensed my stomach muscles and breathed in, I could almost see the beginnings of a six pack. I never saw Tina at the gym.

I was feeling better about myself, but the house was still too quiet. I wanted to be welcomed home in the evening. I couldn't imagine living with any person except Tina. But, I reflected, my companion didn't have to be a person. On Saturday afternoon, I drove over to the animal shelter.

I've often heard it said that you don't choose a dog; he chooses you. As I approached the row of enclosures, a large, shaggy black mongrel stood up. He cocked his head in my direction and wagged his tail. Our eyes met. It was love at first sight. His name was Boris. The volunteer who was showing me round said I could change his name if I wanted to. But as I looked at him, I knew he could never be anything except Boris. He was a cross between a Labrador, a sheepdog and a few other breeds. He sat happily in the passenger seat of the car. When we got home, he walked through the house, sniffing everything carefully. Seemingly content with his new surroundings, he jumped onto the couch in the den and went to sleep.

Boris made a big difference to my life. For one thing, he helped me in my project to get into shape. I no longer spent lunch time in the teachers' lounge, drinking coffee and eating cookies. Instead, I jumped into the car and drove home to take Boris for a run in the park. When I got home in the evening, he jumped up and down like he hadn't seen me in a year. Tina had always seemed pleased to see me when I came home, but she'd restricted herself to, 'Hey, babe.' She'd never jumped up and licked my face. Instead of having Tina's legs across my knees while I was watching TV, I now had a large dog.

At first, I made a rule that the bedroom was the one part of the house where he wasn't allowed. He soon showed me what he thought of that rule. When I was going upstairs to bed, he ran past me and put his head up against the bedroom door. I couldn't open the door without letting him in. He bounded into the bedroom and curled up on the bed. He didn't smell as nice as Tina. But the bed was a lot warmer with him lying beside me. He was also a good guard dog: he barked furiously whenever anyone came near the house. No one was going to break in while he was around.

ONE SUNDAY EVENING, I heard the gate open. Someone was coming up the drive. Boris didn't bark. His tail started wagging and he ran around in an excited little circle. I wasn't expecting anyone. I opened the door.

Tina was standing outside. 'Can I come in?' she said.

Chapter Fourteen

'OF COURSE,' I SAID, standing aside. Tina stepped in. Boris put his front paws on her chest and licked her face.

'I didn't realize you had company,' she said.

'This is Boris.'

She patted him on the head. 'Hello, Boris. You're beautiful.' She looked up at me. 'Are you keeping him for someone?'

'No, he's mine.'

'Were you planning on telling me that we have a dog?'

'I wasn't sure there still was a "we." ' She didn't say anything so I carried on, 'I wasn't sure how you'd react. You've always been more of a cat person.'

'I like dogs too. He's lovely. But … why?'

'I wanted some company.'

She nodded. 'I know that feeling.' She put her coat on the hook where she'd always hung it. She went into the den and sat down on the couch. 'I am too stupid to live,' she said.

'I wouldn't say that,' I said, sitting down next to her.

'I would. What did I think was going to happen if I moved in with Steve?'

'It's not working out?'

'Of course it's not working out.'

It seemed that Tina had her own inner Avril screaming, 'What the hell were you thinking?'

'I thought you liked the guy.'

'He was okay to chat to in the office. But that's not the same as living with someone.'

'And you have great sex.'

'That's just it. I was cock-struck.' She looked round the room. She saw all the stuff we'd accumulated over the years. Then she said, 'He takes his coffee with milk.'

'What a bastard.'

'You take it black. It just felt so wrong being with someone who takes it with milk. And the other day, we were watching a crime drama on TV. I tried getting him to join in with, "I do not have high hopes for his future" but he just couldn't get it right.'

'He's not me.'

'No, he isn't. And the truth is, whenever he had his clothes on, I was bored out of my mind.'

Boris came in. One look at us sitting on the couch together and he jumped up and lay across both our knees. He sighed contentedly as if he'd found the perfect place to lie.

'So what are you going to do?' I asked her.

'I don't know.'

'Are you still with Steve?'

'I've taken all my stuff out of his place.'

'How did you leave things with him?'

She looked down at Boris and tickled him behind the ear. 'I didn't really.'

'What do you mean?'

'I was a coward. He went to a football game with his friends today. I got to thinking. The more I thought, the more I wanted to see you.'

'I'm glad you did.'

'It didn't take me long to pack my bags. I left him a note

saying I needed some time to myself. Anyway, I just wanted to see you. I'll see if I can find a hotel I can check into for a couple of days.'

'You're not going to any hotel. You're staying here.'

'Would that be okay?'

'If Boris agrees.'

Boris lifted his head and licked her face.

'That's settled, then,' I said.

Tina joined me in my healthy dinner of rice and steamed vegetables. She ate it and said it was delicious but added, 'Maybe we should go to the store tomorrow.' When the first crime drama came on TV, we were a bit self-conscious as we shouted, 'I do not have high hopes for his future!' We were trying to convince ourselves that things were back to normal.

I didn't know how Boris would react when it was time to go to bed. There wasn't room for three of us in the bed. He padded up the stairs in front of me, as usual. But when we got to the bedroom door, he just lay down on the landing. 'Make sure you don't step on him if you're going to the bathroom,' I told Tina.

'I'd never do anything to hurt this guy,' she said.

We closed the door behind us. 'Do you hate me?' she asked.

'No.'

'You should. First I abandon you. Then I come back here unannounced.'

'You felt "like dropping in and just expect me to be free"?'

'Exactly. You could have told me to go to hell.'

'But I didn't.'

'You're either very stupid or still in love with me.'

'Or both.'

'That's always a possibility. But I can't really come back here and act like nothing's changed.'

'Maybe things have changed. Perhaps this was something you needed to do. If you've got it out of your system, we can move on.'

'So what do we do now?'

'I think we should make love.'

She didn't say anything. She just unbuttoned her blouse. She smiled at me and paused for a teasing moment just before she reached behind her back to unfasten her bra. 'Did you think you'd never see these again?' she asked. The bra fell away. She took off her jeans and panties. She stood in front of me, naked. 'Everything you remembered?'

'The impossible has happened. You've gotten even more beautiful.'

As I took off my shirt, her eyes widened. 'So have you. Someone's been going to the gym.' We lay down on the bed together. She ran her hands over my arms and shoulders. I knew I still wasn't as big as Steve, but she was enjoying the changes in my body. I kissed my way from her lips down her neck to her breasts. I moved down her body, kissing her stomach. She parted her legs. I licked her cunt, tasting again the sweet, slightly metallic tang of her clit. 'Your tongue feels good,' she said. 'But I want more. I want cock.'

The pack of condoms was still beside the bed. I put one on and slid my cock into Tina's cunt. It felt so good that I came immediately. 'That's one thing that hasn't changed,' I said, sadly.

'It doesn't matter,' she said.

For a couple of weeks, just having Tina back in my bed was enough. I had no problem becoming aroused. But then one night my cock stayed resolutely flaccid, no matter what she did. 'Did I ever tell you about the first time I cheated on you?' she asked me.

'You told Steve you'd never cheated on me.'

'I told Steve a lot of things. How long do you think it was after we got married that I cheated on you?'

'A year, two years?' I said.

'Try half an hour. I never told you about Karl, did I?'

'Karl?'

'All the time we were engaged, all the time we were preparing for the wedding, why do you think I was so calm? At least once a day, I slipped away and met up with Karl. And you remember me saying you can have great sex with someone you hate? Well, I hated Karl. He was an arrogant jerk. But that didn't stop my whole body aching for him all the time.

'He was with me in the hotel room on the very night before our wedding. He fucked me so many times that I thought I'd be too sore to make love to you on our wedding night. But even better is what happened after the ceremony. You remember I slipped away half an hour afterwards. Karl and I had our own ceremony. I held his cock in my hand and said, "I take thee for my unlawful lover, to have and to fuck from this day forward." He got me on the bed on all fours. He lifted up my wedding dress and fucked me from behind. He said, "With this cock, I thee fuck." ' She stopped. 'Is this working for you?' she asked.

I should have loved what she was saying. But it wasn't working. The problem was that I knew it wasn't real. Tina and I had been inseparable in the months leading up to our wedding. There was no way she could have slipped away every day to meet her lover. And on our wedding day, she was out of my sight for a total of about two minutes while she went to the bathroom.

'No, sorry,' I said.

'It's not doing it for me, either. I don't know why.'

'I guess it's hard to go back to fantasy after you've had reality. It's like trying to get drunk on beer if you've gotten used to whiskey.'

'I suppose whatever I do with Darrell, Andrew and Ginny … or Karl will never match what you saw me do with Steve.'

'Shall we try something a bit different?'

'Like what?'

'Do you want to hear what I got up to while you were away?'

'I thought you just sat at home and pined for me.'

'Not every night.'

She smirked. 'Okay, babe, tell me what you were doing.'

'Well, you know Danielle at work?'

'Yes, you pointed her out to me at the party last Christmas.'

'Well, she asked me out to dinner. We went to this nice little Italian restaurant. I had the penne in arrabiata sauce and she had—'

'I don't need this much detail, babe.'

'You described the entire floor plan of Steve's apartment.'

'Yes, all right. What did she have?'

'She had thinly sliced beef with rocket and Parmesan. We drank quite a bit of Valpolicella—'

'What year?'

'And she asked me to walk her home. When we got to her apartment—'

'Studio? Duplex? Loft?'

'When we got to her apartment, she couldn't keep her hands off me. She wanted me so bad. But I took my time.'

'*You* took your time?'

'I slowly undressed her, revealing her beautiful tits.'

'Were they nicer than mine?'

I had to make a quick decision about what she wanted me to say. 'No, they weren't nicer than yours.' She nodded. I'd made the right decision. 'But they were different. She had these brown nipples. I took one into my mouth and sucked it. She was moaning.'

'In a French accent?'

'Her accent drove me wild. I lifted her skirt. She wasn't wearing any panties. She had this thick bush of black hairs—'

'Did you need a machete to get through them?'

'I put two fingers inside her. She was very wet for my cock. I lay down on the bed. She sat on my cock. It felt so good.'

'Were you thinking about me?'

'All I could think about was this hot, tight cunt riding up and down on my cock. I fucked her good and made her cum and then …. Is this working for you?'

'Not really. Hearing about you with other women has never really done it for me. And you're always telling me that fantasies need to be plausible.'

'What do you mean?'

'I love you, babe. But Danielle? A bit out of your league, don't you think?'

'Stranger things have happened.'

My conscience was a bit clearer. It felt good to confess what had happened with Danielle – even if Tina didn't believe me. But we still had a problem. I was lying in bed with my wife. My cock was small and limp. And none of the tricks we normally used were working.

'So, what do we do?' asked Tina. 'Live together like brother and sister? You can spend your evenings surfing online porn. I'll be having fun with the power shower.'

'I think you need a bit more than that.'

'What else can we do?'

'I don't know.'

'Well, you really enjoyed watching me having sex with another man, didn't you?'

'Yes, but—'

'So maybe we need to find some other guy.'

'I don't know, Tina. After what we went through—'

'It was our first time. We made some rookie mistakes. It was someone from work. That was crazy.'

'I did warn you.'

'And you were right. It'll be a lot less awkward with a stranger. The other mistake we made was sticking to the same person. Steve saw me so many times, he started thinking I was his girlfriend. So maybe we don't need to find some other guy. We need to find some other *guys*. We could put a personal ad somewhere: "Attractive married woman seeks men for uncomplicated sex." We'd probably have to hire a couple of secretaries to deal with all the replies.

'Just think about that, babe. I'd have a different man every night. You'd be married to Tina the Super Slut. And we wouldn't bring them back here. We'd go back to our original plan. Anonymous meetings in sleazy motel rooms. You'd watch me getting fucked by the light of the big neon sign in the parking lot. How do you like that idea?'

'Well ....'

'Put it another way ... how's your cock right now?'

'Very hard.'

'Fuck me, then. Fuck me and then we'll start planning our next adventure.'

Chapter Fifteen

~

THE NEXT DAY WAS Saturday. We were on the computer, looking at possible websites where we could advertise when the phone rang. Tina picked it up. 'Oh, hi Louise,' she said. 'How's it going?' Her face fell. 'Oh no! I'm so sorry!' She went quiet for a while. Then she said, 'Yes, of course, I'll meet you there at seven.' She put the phone down and turned to me. 'Louise and Nathan have split up.'

'You're kidding. They've been together longer than we have. What happened?'

'I don't know exactly. She just said he's been working away a lot.'

'Working away or playing away?'

'I'll find out later. Can you fend for yourself tonight, babe? She wants a shoulder to cry on.'

'No problem. Boris and I can have a boys' night in.'

'You're going to play poker and have a few beers with your dog?'

'Something like that.'

Tina left the house at half past six. Even though I was very happy she was back with me, I liked the idea of a quiet evening with Boris. But at eleven o'clock, she still hadn't come home. I tried her cell but there was no answer. She finally came back just before midnight.

'Everything okay?' I asked her.

'You were right about one thing,' she said. 'Nathan has been playing away. He's having an affair with someone at work.'

'No good can come of that.'

'Louise wanted to talk about it. But that's not all she wanted to do tonight.'

'What do you mean?'

'She was out for revenge.'

'Oh dear.'

'I thought we'd just go for a drink somewhere. But she dragged me to this club. When we first arrived, I thought we were the only people there over twenty. And I started thinking things like: why does the music have to be so loud? I felt like such an old woman.

'Louise got onto the dance floor. She might as well have stripped off and told the men to form an orderly queue. She was flirting with every guy in the place. And if none of them had gone for it, I think she'd have started on the women. She danced with this guy who was about twenty-five. At least he could buy his own drinks. She brought him back to the table where I was sitting. He didn't say much, but that could have been because Louise spent the rest of the night trying to lick his tonsils. I sat there, watching the people on the dance floor. Oh babe, did we look that stupid when we were their age?'

'Probably.'

'I was quite relieved when this guy came up to the table and asked me to dance.'

'What did you say?'

'I said yes. I was happy to leave the face suckers to it.'

'Who was he?'

'He was older than most of the people there. Maybe in his thirties. He had blond hair. He was in good shape – big shoulders, broad chest. He said he was in the Air Force. He also said his Porsche was parked outside. He asked me if I wanted to go for a ride.'

'You didn't fall for that old line, did you?'

'Believe me, babe, I just wanted to get out of there. I said goodbye to Louise, but I don't think she even noticed I was leaving. I went out to the parking lot with this guy. He had some sort of sports car, but it definitely wasn't a Porsche. We got in and went for a drive. It just happened to take us back to his place.' She stopped and looked at me. 'Are you okay? You're shaking.'

'Tina, have you any idea how dangerous that was? You meet some random guy in a club. And you just get into his car. You could have been killed.'

'You watch too many crime dramas, Rob. Things like that don't happen in real life.'

'I also watch the news. And yes, they do happen in real life.'

'If something's on the news, it means it doesn't happen very often. Do you want to hear what happened next?'

'I'm not sure. I guess so.'

'Well, we arrived back at his place. I was a bit suspicious when I got there. It was just an ordinary apartment. It wasn't on an Air Force base or anything. And I couldn't see anything in there to suggest he was an airman. There were no pictures on the wall of him and his buddies posing next to a plane. When he went to the bathroom, I took a quick look in his closet. I couldn't see a uniform or anything with Air Force insignia on it.'

'So, not just a stranger, but a stranger who suffers from delusions.'

'I don't think he's delusional. It's probably just a line he uses to pick up women.'

'It obviously works.'

'Anyway, he came back from the bathroom. We kissed a little

bit, but he wasn't really into kissing. He put his hand down my trousers and felt my pussy. He told me to get naked, so I took my clothes off. He didn't bother taking his off. He just pulled his trousers and shorts down. We didn't make it to the bed. He just laid me down on the floor. I was already wet, so he didn't waste any time on foreplay. He just put a condom on and got on top of me. It was good sex. He didn't make me cum, but he had a decent-sized cock and he kept going for quite a while. I enjoyed it. I was hoping he'd finish me off with his tongue, but no such luck. As soon as he'd cum, he just said, "Well, you'll be wanting to get back to your friend." He didn't even offer to drive me home, so I had to call a taxi.'

'I can't believe this,' I said.

'What? We agreed that I'd start seeing lots of different people.'

'We agreed we'd place a couple of ads, go through all the replies, and find someone suitable for you. That's very different from letting a guy treat you like that.'

'I respect him in a way.'

'He doesn't respect you very much.'

'At least he was honest.'

'By pretending to be in the Air Force?'

'That's not what I mean. He didn't come out with any bullshit like, "I'm expecting a phone call from Tokyo, so you'd better go." He didn't even say, "I'll call you." He didn't pretend it was anything except a quick fuck on the floor. Look on the bright side. At least we don't need to worry that he's going to fall in love with me.'

'That's very comforting.'

'Do you want to fuck me now?'

'No, I'm still shaking.'

'Babe, I was fine. I trust my instincts. And my instincts said it would be okay.'

I got ready for bed. Maybe Tina was right. Maybe a regular diet of crime dramas had blown my fear of stranger danger out of all proportion. But I still wanted to protect her. I went into the bedroom. Tina was already in bed. 'Next time you go out to meet someone,' I said, 'I'm coming with you.'

Chapter Sixteen

~

TINA STARTED GETTING READY at five o'clock. She sat in the bath and asked me to shave her legs. I ran my hand down her left leg. 'I'm not sure they need it.'

'Do them anyway. I want to be at my best.'

'You've never worried about things like this before.'

'It's been a long time since I've gone out to pick someone up. The last time was an accident.'

'You *accidentally* went home with a guy and had sex on his floor?'

'You know what I mean. I went out that night to comfort Louise.'

'You didn't even take this much trouble for Steve.'

'He'd seen me crawling into work on a Monday morning. There was no point trying to fool him that I'm some glamour puss.'

'Did you shave your legs for me?'

'You'd seen me around campus in my jeans and an old sweater. There was no fooling you, either.'

'You looked great.'

'Well, I've got to look even greater tonight.'

When her legs were perfectly smooth, she got out of the bath and toweled herself down.

She doesn't normally wear much makeup. When she's going to work she just wears eyeliner and sometimes a subtle shade of lipstick. But she hunted through her drawer and found a bottle of bright red nail varnish. Still naked, she sat down. She painted her nails carefully and then flapped her hands. 'How do you tell if they're dry?' she asked.

'I don't know. I've never worn nail varnish.'

'If I touch one of my nails and it smudges, I guess it wasn't dry.' She flapped her hands for a bit longer, then blew on her nails. She tentatively touched one. It didn't smudge. 'How do they look?'

'Scarlet for a scarlet lady.'

She grinned. She found a lot of things in her drawer that I didn't know she had – mascara, eye shadow, lipstick that matched her nails. She put it all on carefully.

I generally prefer Tina's natural good looks, but I had to admit she looked sexy, wearing nothing except her makeup. She put on a pair of black panties and a black see-through bra. Though she made a show of looking through the clothes in her closet, I think she'd already decided what she was going to wear. She picked out a black dress and stepped into it. 'Can you zip me up, babe? You probably won't be the one unzipping me later.' She looked stunning. There wasn't any doubt about it. I wouldn't be the one unzipping her. She could have any man she wanted.

'What are *you* going to wear?' she asked.

'It doesn't matter. No one's going to be looking at me.'

'True. Let's go.'

I'd already told her that I'd do the driving. She could have a couple of drinks to get into the party mood, but I was going to stay sharp. I wanted to be able to step in if she found herself in any trouble. 'Do you know where you want to go?' I asked her.

'Yes. Turn left at the lights.'

We drove about thirty miles out of town. Tina told me to turn into the car park of a square, concrete building. It looked more like a warehouse than a bar. But I could hear music coming through the open door.

We walked in. The room was dimly lit. It took a moment for my eyes to adjust. At one of the tables was a group of guys. They were all dressed as construction workers. Some other men were dressed as cops. At another table were guys dressed as firemen. 'What are we doing here?' I whispered to Tina. 'This is a gay bar.'

'No, it's not. Can't you see everyone looking at me?'

'So these guys are *really* cops and firemen?'

'They're probably lawyers and accountants. I read about this place online. It's where women go to fulfill their fantasies about men in uniform.'

'So where are these women?'

She looked round the bar. 'Good point. Maybe the word hasn't got out to many women yet. I'm liking my chances.'

I bought a white wine for Tina and a Coke for me. She drank her wine quickly. She was excited but nervous. A lot of the men were looking at her. 'Okay,' she said, squeezing my hand under the table, 'let's do this.'

She started to get up, but I stopped her. 'Just one thing,' I asked. 'Who am I?'

'What do you mean?'

'Am I your brother? Your gay best friend?'

'You're my husband. You're here to watch me getting fucked by another man because it turns you on. It's best to be honest.'

It was strange to talk about being honest in a place like this. There was a small dancing area in the middle of the room. It was empty. Tina stepped onto it. All eyes were on her as she started to move to the music. I was reminded again of just how sexy she is. I could see the guys talking to each other. They were talking about her. It was exciting, knowing that my wife was the center of attention for so many men. But I also felt exposed and vulnerable. What would I do if things went bad? How could I protect her from a room full of cops and firemen?

A guy went up to her. He didn't say anything. He just started dancing in front of her. I thought he looked all right. He was dressed as a cop. He was quite tall. He had brown hair, a beard and an earring in his left ear. I thought she could do worse. But she waved him away with a smile and a shake of her head.

She looked a lot more interested in the next guy, who had very short blond hair and blue eyes. He was dressed as a fireman, but without a jacket. He wore red suspenders over a shirt in coarse blue fabric.

They danced together. My heart was thumping as a slow song came on and she put her arms around his neck. He put his arms round her waist and pulled her towards him. She smiled at me over his shoulder. I was glad she was making me part of it. As they danced, his hands strayed down to touch her ass. She pressed her hips into his thighs. He took her face between his hands. She looked up at him, her eyes flashing with desire. As he moved his face towards hers, she parted her lips. She closed her eyes and lost herself in the kiss.

I saw her whisper something in his ear. He looked over at me with a puzzled expression. Then he gave a small shrug. He whispered something back to her. She took his hand and led him towards our table. 'This is my husband,' she said.

She didn't say anything more. 'Nice to meet you,' I said. 'And you are …?'

'We've decided not to worry about names,' said Tina. 'This is just the guy I'm going to be with tonight.'

'Have you got a place?' he asked.

'We're only in town for one night,' she lied. 'We're staying with a friend. She doesn't really understand our lifestyle. So, if it's okay with you, let's go to a motel.'

'Fine by me,' he said.

The three of us went outside and got into the car. 'I know the perfect place,' said Tina. 'Turn right out of here, babe. I'll give you directions.'

Tina had been busy on the internet, scoping out places. She'd found a motel straight out of her fantasies, right down to the sign in the parking lot – red and yellow flashing neon. Checking in was just like Tina had said. I gave our name as the Smiths, but the desk clerk didn't even look up.

Tina was also right about another thing: it *was* less awkward with a stranger. There was no stilted conversation, no sitting around wondering who was going to make the first move. As soon as the door was shut, he kissed Tina on the lips. She closed her eyes and enjoyed the feeling of these new lips against hers.

There were two beds in the room. I sat on the one farthest from the door. He put his hand under her dress. Eyes still closed, she moaned as his hand snaked into her panties.

'How do you like it when I do this?' he asked. 'Scale of one to ten?'

Tina opened her eyes and frowned. She hadn't been expecting that question. She wasn't sure how to answer. I'm sure he was hoping to hear, 'Ten, eleven – off the scale.' But she decided to be honest. 'About a seven.'

He didn't look disappointed. He just doubled his efforts. 'What needs to happen to make it a ten?' he asked.

'Why don't you use your tongue?' she suggested.

He laid her gently on the bed. He pushed the hem of her dress up to her waist and pulled down her panties. I wanted him to take a moment to appreciate the beauty of my wife's cunt. It was the first time he'd seen it. But he didn't pause for a second. He just got onto his knees and started licking. She threw her head back on the bed and gave herself up to the feeling. Her moans were getting louder. I thought there was a chance he'd make her cum. But then he stopped and asked her again, 'How about that? Scale of one to ten?'

'Nine,' she said.

'What needs to happen to make it a ten?'

I'm sure she wanted to say, 'You need to shut up and get on with it.' But instead she said, 'I need a cock for a perfect ten.'

She watched him as he took his clothes off. She was happy with what she saw. His chest was covered with blond hairs. I wasn't sure how she'd react to that. I don't have a particularly hairy body. Neither does Steve. She seemed to enjoy the novelty. She ran her hand through his chest hair. He pushed the straps off her shoulders and pulled down her dress. He didn't even stop when he saw her tits looking gorgeous in the black see-through bra. He just stood up and reached into his jacket pocket.

He took a condom out of his wallet. He'd come to the bar prepared. He took off his trousers and shorts. Tina saw him naked for the first time. Though not as big as Steve's, his cock was a reasonable size. I guessed it was about as big as mine. Tina's dress had been pushed up from the bottom and pulled down from the top, leaving it bunched awkwardly around her middle. She stood up and slipped it off. 'Bra on or off?' she asked him.

'Whatever you like,' he said.

She took it off. As he lay on top of her, she reached down for his cock and put it inside her. He started fucking her, and he looked like he knew what he was doing. She pushed her tits up so his chest hairs rubbed against them. After a couple of minutes, he asked again, 'Scale of one to ten?'

Tina sighed. She was getting annoyed, but she was still more turned-on than angry. 'It's definitely a ten now. Stop worrying. Just fuck me.'

He carried on fucking her. She arched her back and moaned. She shouted, 'Yes! Yes! Yes!' and sank her head back into the pillow, grinning happily. He looked pleased, but I knew her better than he did. Soon after that, he came inside her.

'How was that overall?' he asked her.

'You did just fine,' she said, as she climbed back into her dress.

We dropped him off near the bar. 'Have a good one,' he said, as he got out of the car.

We drove off. Tina laughed. 'So how was that for you, babe?' she asked. 'Scale of one to ten?'

'What was that about?'

'We do ongoing appraisals at work. But I've never done one during sex before. I couldn't really get into it when he was fucking me. I was just waiting for him to ask the question again.'

'I'd give him a six.'

'A bit harsh.'

'Firm but fair. I wanted him to appreciate you more.'

She nodded and gave a little shrug. 'He was only interested in his own performance. Actually, I quite liked the way he just got on with it. I'll give him an eight. He gets an extra point for getting out of the car without suggesting we meet again or asking for my phone number. He understands what casual sex is all about.'

'So the actual sex was only a seven.'

'I guess so.'

'Why did you fake it?'

'You noticed that, did you?'

'I'm your husband.'

'I didn't want him to try making me cum going "Scale of one to ten?" the whole time. It was easier to pretend he'd already done it.'

'He's quite a hairy guy. Did you like that?'

'Yes, I did. Normally, I drink white wine. Sometimes, a glass of red is great. Variety is the spice of life. And I suppose that's what I'm going to get now. Hairy, smooth, dark hair, blond hair, no hair.' My cock twitched at the thought of her with all those different men. 'His cock wasn't up there with Steve's,' she carried on.

'I reckoned it was about the same as mine.'

'I suppose so. But at least he knew what to do with it.'

'Was he better than me?'

'Oh yes. Not as good as Steve. But a lot better than you.'

'So what would you give me? Scale of one to ten?'

'Two and a half on a good day.'

'And on a bad day?'

'Is there a minus scale?'

I couldn't wait until we got home. We were passing the woods where we go walking. Driving into the parking lot, I parked in the corner farthest from the road. Tina lay down on the back seat of the car. I lay on top of her. I didn't care about the police. I didn't care if anyone could see us. I fucked her hard and fast. Neither of us was surprised that it didn't take long. But I could hear the lust in Tina's voice as she said, 'We haven't done that in a while.'

'I needed to fuck you.'

'I'm glad you did. That was almost a five.' I moved down her body. I had to roll myself into a tight ball with my feet and my butt jammed against the car door, but I managed to get my tongue onto her clit. I licked her quickly. After being fucked by two men in less than an hour, she didn't need much to make her cum. She let out a scream and her ass bucked against the back seat of the car. She wasn't faking this time. 'That was a ten, babe,' she said.

I got back into the driver's seat and drove us home.

THE NEXT DAY, TINA was a bit less positive. 'I'm not sure I want to do that again.'

'It's up to you.'

'In a way, it was quite hot, picking up a guy in a bar. But do I really want to do it every night?'

'It doesn't have to be every night.'

'And it wasn't that great, really. It's not his fault. Apart from all the "scale of one to ten" stuff, he didn't do anything wrong. It's just usually not that great the first time with anyone.'

'Bit of a problem if you want to focus on one night stands.'

'I know. We might have to face the fact that there's only one person who can really fuck me right,' she said.

'And who's that?' I asked, even though I already knew the answer.

'Steve.'

'But you can't start things up with him again.'

'Why not?'

'He'll just get hung up on you again.'

'It'll be different this time. Maybe we won't let him stay the night.'

'We didn't *let* him stay the night last time. He just did it.'

'We can set Boris on him.'

'I'd pay to see that.'

'Maybe I won't let him kiss me – Steve, I mean. Boris can kiss me whenever he wants. Actually, no, Steve's a good kisser. I want to kiss him again. But I want you to know something, babe. I love you. That time away from you made me realize just how much. I'm never going to walk out on you again.'

'Promise?'

'Promise. The real mistake I made was having sex with him when you weren't there. That should never have been part of it. We need to explain to him that you're going to be there every time from now on. It's just as much about you and me as it is about me and him. The only thing he can expect from me is the best sex of his life. So let's start over. I'll see if he wants to go for a drink after work tomorrow.'

Just then, Boris jumped off our knees and ran out into the hall. He started barking at the front door. 'What's with him?' asked Tina.

'It means there's someone outside.'

'You'd better check.'

I got up and went to the front door. I held on to Boris's collar as I opened the door. He rose up on his hind paws and strained forward, still barking loudly. There was a dark figure at the end of the driveway. I knew who it was immediately. When he saw the door opening, he ducked behind the hedge.

I shut the door and went to get Boris a chew treat. I was pleased with him for scaring Steve away. Boris wouldn't come back into the den. He sat by the front door, growling. 'Come on, Boris,' I said. 'He's gone now.' Boris didn't move. 'He must still be out there.'

Tina sighed. 'Tell him to come in.'

'I don't think Boris would like that.'

'If he's going to start coming over on weekends again, Boris will have to get used to him.'

I shut Boris in the kitchen and opened the front door. I could see the top of Steve's head bobbing about behind the hedge. 'Come in, Steve,' I called. 'Tina wants to talk to you.' The head disappeared. I waited for a few moments, but I didn't see him again. I went back inside.

'What's he doing?' asked Tina.

'Congratulations. You've got a stalker.' I let Boris out of the kitchen. He ran to the door and sniffed the air. He immediately started barking again. 'He's still there.'

She stood up. 'Let me talk to him.' She went to the door. 'Steve,' she shouted, 'quit messing around. Come inside and let's talk.'

Steve came out from behind the hedge and walked slowly up the drive. 'Sorry, buddy,' I muttered to Boris, as I put him back in the kitchen and shut the door.

Steve reached the door. 'Where's the dog?'

'Don't worry about him,' I said.

'I don't like dogs.'

'Too bad. He lives here now.'

'Did you get him just to keep me away?'

'Not everything revolves around you.'

'Sit down, Steve,' said Tina. He sat down. 'How are you?'

'Not too good. My girlfriend skipped out on me without having the guts to tell it to my face.'

'I'm not your girlfriend. I've never been your girlfriend.'

'You were living in my apartment and sleeping in my bed. You sure acted like my girlfriend.'

'I know. I'm sorry. That was a mistake. I'm Rob's wife. He's the one I want to be with.'

'So I've done my job and now you can toss me in the trash?'

'We're hoping it doesn't come to that. Rob and I have been discussing it. Why can't we go back to the way things were before? You come round here every now and then and we have great sex. You don't need to start talking about girlfriends.'

'So you want me to be your personal gigolo – just some guy who fucks you every now and then?'

'It won't be like that.'

'If you're going to treat me like a prostitute, are you going to pay me like one?'

'Don't be silly, Steve. We're friends.'

'And you think he's going to watch?'

'Yes. From now on, he's going to watch every time. We've decided that's a crucial part of it for us.'

'You've got it all sorted out, then?'

'We think it's the best solution for all of us.'

'Do you? Well, I've got another solution.' He put his hand into his pocket and took out an envelope. 'I just came round to give you this. Wait till I've gone before you read it.'

He walked out, slamming the front door behind him. I let Boris out of the kitchen. He ran to the front door, sniffed and then lay down. Steve had gone.

Tina ripped open the envelope. Before she'd read half of it, she said, 'Oh, shit.'

'What?' I asked.

She didn't say anything more until she'd finished reading it. Then she handed it to me.

"Dear Tina," it read, "It was terrible to come home and find the apartment empty. I assume you've gone back to your husband. I know you will come back to me, because I can take you to places inside yourself that you will never find if you stay with Rob. You have a strong need to be dominated. Rob can never fulfill this need because he's not strong enough. Only I am strong enough. Deep down, you know this to be true. But you may be in denial. So you may need some encouragement to take the path that is ultimately right for you. I would remind you that I still have those photos that Rob and I took of you. If you do not agree to all the terms stated in the contract below, everyone in the company will see these photos. Please understand that I love you and it's not my intention to threaten you. I just want to encourage you to do what you know in your heart is best for you."

'What's this crap about a contract?' I asked.

'Someone's been reading *Fifty Shades of Grey.*' She handed me another sheet of paper.

"I, Tina Matthews, will make myself sexually available to Steve Henderson at all times and will perform any sex act that he requires. I will live with Steve permanently or until he asks me to leave. I can visit Rob Matthews only with Steve's permission. As my body now belongs to Steve, I accept that all sexual contact with Rob is prohibited. If Rob wishes to watch me having sex with Steve, he must pay a fee. Price to be determined."

There was a space at the bottom for her signature. I gave it back to her. She read it again and said quietly to herself, '"…will perform any sex act that he requires."' Just for a moment, I thought she might be considering going along with it. But then her eyes hardened and she said, 'Fuck that! We'll show him he can't threaten us.'

'Absolutely.'

'And what does he mean? I have a "strong need to be dominated"? It's not like I've ever asked him to spank me or anything.'

'No, but you did want to hear about how that other woman was better than you. That might suggest a desire to be humiliated. And you did give your breasts to him as a present.'

'Only for the weekend. There's a big difference between that and wanting to be a full-time sex slave.'

'You're definitely not the "Yes, master" type. Do you honestly think he'd show the photos to everyone in the company?'

'I don't know. He seems pretty worked up. There's no telling what he might do.'

'We can't let people see those photos.'

'So people would see me naked. It would be embarrassing. But it wouldn't be the end of my career.'

I took her by the shoulders. 'Tina, you're not just naked in those photos. They went a lot further than that. If the people at work saw them, you *would* have to resign.'

'But he's in those photos as well. He'd have to resign too.'

'I'm not sure any of the photos showed his face. Even the ones where he's licking you are close-ups on his tongue.'

'You warned me those photos were a bad idea. You were right. I'm going to have to quit my job, aren't I?'

She threw this out quite casually. She didn't realize what an impact it would have on our lives. It had been tough supporting Boris and me on my salary. I would really struggle to support all three of us. And times were hard. She couldn't be sure of getting another job. 'Don't do anything hasty,' I said. 'We need to think about what to do.'

'I don't see what we can do.'

I had already thought of something. But I didn't say anything because I knew she wasn't going to like it.

THE NEXT MORNING, I got out of bed before the alarm went off and went out of the bedroom, closing the door quietly behind me. Boris was lying on the landing. He lifted his head and raised an eyebrow as I passed. He knew I was up to something. I went downstairs and into the hallway. Tina's coat was hanging up by the door. I felt in her pocket and found her phone. I went through her list of contacts and found the number I wanted. I copied the number to my phone.

Chapter Seventeen

~

W HEN TINA CAME HOME that evening, she sat down and said, 'I think I know what he's planning.'

'What?'

'He came up to my desk and just said, "Well …?" No good morning or anything, just "Well …?" No one else was around so I told him straight out he could go fuck himself. He just sneered and said, "In that case, I hope you're looking forward to the ball. I'm giving a breakdown of the annual figures. I've got some stunning visuals." He walked off before I could say anything.'

'But that'll get him fired. I'm sure it's against company policy to put on a porn show at the annual ball.'

'He's not thinking about that. And maybe he doesn't care. Maybe that rich aunt of his can help him out if he loses his job.'

'So what do you want to do?'

'I'll tell you what we're going to do. We're going to the ball. And if he shows those pictures, we'll just get up and dance. I'm going to dance around the room in my husband's arms. We'll show everyone just how much we love each other. And what if

I do lose my job? People have brought up big families on less than what you earn. We'll be fine.'

I wasn't so sure about this. But I nodded. 'Yes, of course we will.'

'So are we going to let anyone intimidate us? Hell, no!'

'Hell, no!' I agreed.

On the evening of the ball, Tina put on a white see-through bra and panties set. It felt good, knowing that she was wearing them for me this time. Whatever happened at the ball, I'd be the one taking those off that night. I got out the suit I normally wore only for weddings. Tina helped me with my tie. She put on a scarlet silk dress. 'I may as well look the part.'

'You look stunning. I don't care what anyone else thinks of you. I'm proud to be with you tonight.'

The taxi arrived five minutes early and took us to a restaurant at the edge of town. The top floor of the restaurant was the function room. Tables were laid out round the dance floor. There was a stage at one end of the room. I saw David on the stage, talking to someone who looked like the sound man. There was a big screen behind him. I went over to the bar, located along one side of the room, and got us a couple of glasses of champagne. We moved around the room, chatting to people. Everyone said Tina looked great. I recognized some people I'd met at the same function the year before. And I met a lot of people for the first time. I explained what I did for a living at least ten times.

Then I saw Steve. He was standing by the bar with a bottle of beer. He finished his beer and came up to us. 'Good evening,' he said. He wasn't drunk, but he'd obviously had more than one beer.

'Good evening,' I said. 'It's a nice place, isn't it?'

He ignored me and looked at Tina. 'I want to talk to you.'

'We don't want to talk to you,' she said.

'It's your last chance to save your career.'

She sighed. 'All right. Come on.'

We found a little room off the hallway where the spare tables were stacked up, turned on the light, and shut the door. 'What do you want?' she asked.

'After dinner, David's going to make a speech. Then he's going to hand over to me. My laptop is supposed to have a whole lot of boring graphs and charts on it. It's actually got some very pretty pictures of you. And the pictures are all very clear. No one will be in any doubt that it's you. You will lose your job.'

'So will you.'

'Hey, I was as shocked as everyone else. My laptop's been on the stage all day while we've been setting up. I went out to grab lunch. Anyone could have swapped the pictures round. We'll probably never know who did it. It was stupid of me not to password protect, but I'm not going to get fired for that.'

'So what do you want?'

'You.'

'You still want me to go along with that stupid contract?'

'No, forget the contract. I just want things back the way they were. I want to come round to your place on a Friday night. I want to spend the weekend with you. Then I'll leave on Sunday.'

Not so long ago, this was exactly what Tina had wanted. I thought there was a very real chance that she'd agree. But she didn't even hesitate. 'No way.'

'Why not?'

'You blackmailed us. You threatened us.'

'You hate me. So what? You said you could have great sex with someone you hate. I didn't understand that for a while. I started thinking I must be in love with you. But now I know. All we ever had was great sex. And that's what I want to get back to.'

'Do you remember I also said if I thought you were a bastard, I wouldn't let you in the house?'

'Tina, to me, this is a no-brainer. You keep your job. And you carry on having the best sex you'll ever have.'

'With an extremely modest man.'

He ignored the comment and turned to me. 'And you can keep getting off on watching your wife with a guy who actually knows what he's doing. Everyone wins. So let's make a date for next Friday. And right now, I want you to suck my cock as a sign of good faith. Do that and there'll be nothing on the big screen except graphs and charts.'

'Fuck you,' she said. She opened the door. He made a move towards her. I took a step forwards and stood between them. He raised his hands. Then he stopped. He looked me up and down and realized he couldn't just shove me out of the way. 'Come on, Rob,' said Tina. We went out.

'Good luck finding a new job!' he shouted after us.

Chapter Eighteen

~

I FELT EXHILARATED AS we went back into the main room. Tina squeezed my hand and said, 'No one's going to mess with me while my man's around.'

The room had filled up. There were about two hundred people sitting at the tables or chatting by the bar. We had a good dinner, along with several glasses of champagne. Tina knew the other people at our table and we all chatted freely. We almost forgot what was going to happen next.

We were having our coffee when the room lights went down and the stage lights came up. A couple of people clapped as David rose to his feet. Steve was sitting at the back of the stage with some other people. He looked straight at Tina. Then he looked at me. He was daring us to stay in our seats. We didn't move.

David spoke into the microphone. 'Good evening, ladies and gentlemen. Welcome to our annual company dinner. I know you'll want to join me in thanking the people who have prepared this wonderful meal for us.' Everyone clapped at that. 'It's been a good year for the company. Turnover has increased by six percent. That's two percent more than we projected. And I'm very happy to say that you'll all be receiving bonuses.' This got the biggest round of applause of the evening. 'At this point, I was going to hand over to Steve Henderson for a detailed breakdown of the annual figures.' Steve didn't seem to hear the word "was" and started to get out of his seat. 'But I'm not going to do that,' continued David. Steve sat down again, looking confused. 'Instead, I want to talk to you about the people behind the figures. Many of you, I know, don't like me. I'm always pushing you to do more, work longer hours, get involved in new projects. Some might call me a bully. Some of you, I'm sure, use stronger words than that. But I only do it because I want you to be the best.

'I had a boss once. He came in to the office at ten o'clock every morning with coffee and doughnuts for everyone. In the evening, he took us bowling. We thought he did that because he cared about us. The truth is that he just wanted an easier life for himself. We all liked him. But we were frustrated because we weren't growing.

'I left his team and started working for a new boss. He was on my case twenty-four seven. I hated him. But after a year with him, I was a hundred times better at my job than I'd ever been before. I'm telling you this because I want you to understand that I do care about my people.

'One thing I value in my team is diversity. I would hate to be in a room full of people exactly like me. For example, there's someone in my team who likes fishing. I can't imagine anything more boring than sitting by a river all day, hoping that a fish will come along. I also don't approve of fishing. I think it's cruel. But I would never discriminate against that person, just because I don't understand or approve.' He paused, looked up and caught Tina's eye. 'And I'm sure there are some other people in my team who do things I don't understand or approve of. But I would never allow that person to be mistreated as a result. There is no room in my team for intimidation, harassment or bullying. Well, there might be some bullying but I'll handle that myself. But if I do bully you, it will be to help your development – not because of anything that goes on in your personal life.

'And now I'd like to hand over to Carol Adams, who'll be reviewing the year in Marketing.'

David sat down. Some people clapped. But a lot of them looked puzzled. This was not the speech they'd expected from him. No one was looking more puzzled than Tina. I don't think she heard much of the other speeches. The final speaker told us to have a good time and show some moves on the dance floor. As soon as he sat down, Tina motioned me to follow her. We went out into the hall. 'What happened there?' she asked.

'How should I know?' I said, innocently.

'David deliberately stopped Steve from speaking. It was like he—'

'Ah, Tina!' said a voice behind us. We turned and saw David coming towards us. 'Are you having a good evening?'

'Why did … how did you …?' she stammered.

'You have your husband to thank for that. Rob phoned me up and we met for a drink last Tuesday. We had a very nice little chat.'

She looked at me. 'You told my boss?'

'A good thing he did,' said David. 'If Steve had carried out his threats, I think you'd have found it a little embarrassing to come into work tomorrow. Oh, on that subject, I'm on a teleconference with Beijing at six tomorrow morning. It's a major new client. A lot of the work will probably be coming your way. It would be useful for you to sit in on the call. Is that okay?'

'That's fine,' mumbled Tina.

'If any of those pictures appear online or if you have any further trouble, you'll be sure to let me know, won't you? And I've been thinking for some time that Steve's development might be best served by a move to a different department. What do you think?'

'He doesn't have much room to grow in his current role.'

'My thoughts exactly. Be in by five thirty, so I can brief you about the teleconference. Better not go overboard on the champagne tonight.'

He walked off. She turned to me, too surprised and confused to form a sentence. 'What …? What the …?'

'Every night you came home and complained about David. But you never said that he took credit for your work or put you down in front of your colleagues. He sounded like a tough boss, not a bastard. It was a risk, but I was pretty sure he'd stand up for you.'

'But how am I going to look him in the eye again?'

'You heard what he said in his speech. He doesn't care what people do in their personal lives. And he wants you on an important call with a major new client tomorrow.'

'Why didn't you tell me what you were going to do?'

'I thought you might object.'

'You thought I might object to you telling my boss the intimate details of my sex life? Well, you're right. I'm mad at you for telling him. I'm super mad at you for not telling me first. But—'

'But what?'

'But you are so getting laid tonight. Let's have one dance before we go. I want to dance with my husband in front of everyone.'

LOTS OF PEOPLE WATCHED as we danced. I felt the pride of knowing I was with the most beautiful woman in the room. We didn't take David's advice. I bought a bottle of champagne at the bar, and we drank most of it in the taxi. When we got home, we poured a couple of glasses and toasted each other. Boris wasn't entirely sure what we were celebrating, but he joined in the party, jumping up and licking our faces. But when we went into the bedroom, he lay down quietly on the landing. It might be my imagination, but I think he even winked at me as I closed the door.

I felt like I was Tina's hero. I ripped off her clothes. I laid her down on the bed and fucked her hard.

For almost a minute.

We lay quietly for a moment. 'We still have a problem,' I said sadly.

'It doesn't really matter,' she said. She'd said that before. She hadn't sounded convincing the first time, either.

'You deserve to have good sex.'

'But what can we do?'

'I don't know. You don't want to go with anyone else from work. You don't like picking up men in bars. Do you want to go back to the idea of advertising somewhere?'

'I don't think so. I was talking to Louise the other day. She's still trying to take revenge on Nathan by having sex with every man in the world. So she placed an ad on a couple of sites. She said she got hundreds of replies but most of them just said, " 'Sup?" The really eloquent ones managed, "How you doing?" None of them made any effort to say who they were or what they were looking for. I don't think I can be bothered with a bunch of guys like that.'

'I don't know what else we can do, then.'

'There's one option we haven't considered.'

'What's that?'

'The ex factor.'

'What do you mean?'

'There are a few men out there I've been with before. Some of them were very good back when I knew them. And they've had a few years to work on their technique since then.'

'You want to get back with Nick?'

'Oh no. He's far too jealous. And anyway, he's married now. His wife has my sympathy. He's probably fitted her with a tracking device. But you remember me telling you about Kieran?'

'The one who fucked your tits?'

'Or Kieraned me, as Steve put it. I happened to find him on Facebook.'

'Purely by accident.'

'Of course. I saw some pictures of him. He's still an interesting looking guy.'

'I'm guessing there wasn't a photo of his cock.'

'No, but there was one of him on a beach in just swim shorts. A very impressive bulge. And his relationship status says he's single.'

'You want to send him a message?'

'Well … actually ….'

'You already have, haven't you?'

'I just sent him a "Hi, remember me?" message. He wrote back immediately saying, "Yes, of course I remember you." It turns out he only lives about twenty miles away.'

'You want to meet up with him?'

'Er …. I told him we're free next Friday.'

'Oh, Tina! I wish you'd told me before—'

'How hard is your cock right now?'

'Very hard.'

'Do you want to fuck me again?'

'Yes.'

'Turn the light out.'

ROB MATTHEWS WAS BORN in London. He divides his time between Britain and the United States. He lives with his wife Tina and their dog Boris. Coming soon: Book 2 of the Cuckold Odyssey series.

Follow Rob on Facebook and Twitter:

FB: Rob Matthews Author

Twitter: @robandtina1

Another episode in the Cuckold Odyssey Series will be released in 2017.

In the meantime, go to www.fannypress.com to check out the following titles:

David McManus

The Reluctant Cuckold

Cuck Storm Horizon

Alex Hathaway

From Housewife to Cuckoldress: How I Took Sexual Control of a Marriage in Crisis

The Education of a Cuckold

Derrin Hart

Our Dark Secret: A Modern Cuckold Memoir

Tiffany's Cuckold

Southern Belle Cuckold